W9-AKP-891

Blurred Edges

Kurt Bensworth

PHC Publishing
California

PHC Publishing
Mission Viejo, California

Contact us at PHCpublishing@cox.net

Printed in the United States of America

First Edition: October 2017

PHC Publishing is a division of Pacific Holding Company, LLC. The PHC Publishing name and logo is a trademark of Pacific Holding Company, LLC.

ISBN   978-0-9824547-3-2

Library of Congress Control Number: 2017947619

Jacket design by Angie Vangalis/AV Graphics
Jacket original artwork by Janet Takahashi
Photograph by Conrad Boyse/Peppertree Studios

This book is dedicated to those that have a silent voice.
Yet, can still be heard.

Acknowledgments

Writing is never a solitary endeavor; there are always many people to thank for their time, effort, and ability to complete a novel.

First and foremost, to my editors, Mia Taylor and Flo Selfman, thank you for working so hard on this project and for understanding what this book is all about. Love stories are a difficult genre to write and harder to fit all the pieces together flawlessly. We did it, again.

To my numerous reviewers: Michelle Arcos, Tom Berean, LeAnne Hunt, Jeff Pajak, Peter Jessup, Cathy MacAloney, Krissie McMakin, Steve Ramirez, and Andrea Ring. Your input was invaluable and has been memorialized as partial names of characters or personality traits of a character. I love you all.

To Marilza Rezende Neves Bruinsma, Dave Cherman, Kelly Palmer, and Kathryn Wirzbicki, I'm truly grateful for your thoughts and insight.

Yes, I can't forget my wife, Sandra. More than anything, I am centered because of you and our belief in God. Your understanding and devotion has inspired me to things I couldn't accomplish on my own. Thank you.

Prologue

The heart never lies . . .

"No no no. I'm sorry, please don't go. I didn't mean that," she whimpered with sorrow-filled eyes. Leaning flush against the cold metal door, she begged, "Please, Nicky, come back, take me with you. I'll be good. I really will, I swear." She remained flat behind the door as tears streamed down her face. "Nicky!"

NICK SITS BEHIND his desk rehashing Mary's last words while sipping on another one of his comfort drinks. He has never been the sort of man who could walk away from someone in trouble. Yet, in the midst of Mary's raw, unabashed pleading, he chose to abandon her. Yes, she had lied. But was that reason enough to turn his back so easily, considering how his first wife had chewed him up and spit him out? Still, he had been there for her—always.

Nick cringed. He didn't want to compare Mary to anyone and especially the ex. Nonetheless, he held open the door for Stephanie, despite her betrayals. And then to top it off, tonight walked away from Mary when she needed him most. Why? What kind of man had he become? He didn't know anymore.

He took a long drink and grabbed another sheet of paper and started over.

I don't remember how I got to this point. It's not as if there weren't any signs. There were plenty of them. I should have known better than to ignore what was right in front of me. Then again, never questioning you did provide some solace, but at what price? Me . . . again.

Nick abruptly pulls the pen from the paper. A lone tear gathers on the inside corner of his left eye. It will not fall tonight. They hardly ever do anymore.

Regardless of what others say about him, he is not this stone-faced, coldhearted beast of a man, although he does tend to display the personality traits of being a lifelong detective like a badge of honor—to protect and preserve his heart. And even in his newest job choice, his peers perceive him as aloof—at best, indifferent. He's keenly aware of this façade. Whether out of necessity or habit, he wears a front in the same way he wore his old tin shield—as a thin wall against the outside world.

His underbelly is quite the opposite. He's just remarkably talented at covering up things—simple things—like emotions, feelings. Yet, whenever circumstances require it, he can turn on the magic. Nick can draw nearly anyone into his fold when he speaks. However, it's when he's alone that the real man is revealed—mainly through his prose. During his lifetime he has endured many tragedies. Each one has torn away a small piece of his soul. And after this latest revelation about Mary, there are no more tears. Besides, how can crying undo what is true?

That's why he writes. His mother, a prolific writer and lifelong diarist, had often said, "If you put your pain down on paper, the hurt is left behind in your words." And over the past three years he has accumulated several pounds of writings, on bits of paper of various sizes and shapes. Some of them on napkins; some, barely legible, scrawled on the backs of old household bills and coffee-stained envelopes; but most are on standard, white, lined notepaper, neatly folded in half. He keeps them in the bottom drawer of his desk, and once in the drawer, they are never looked at again. Even so, they stack up, a weighty mass of searing, unbridled thoughts, waiting to be addressed.

The writings have been an exercise in releasing the anger, except it's never really worked for him. Nevertheless, he continues to write, hoping, praying for a resolution to issues of the heart.

Returning pen to paper, he scratches out the word "Me." Frustrated, he picks up the sheet, rips it in two, and throws the pieces on the floor. Grabbing the notepad, he tears off a new sheet, grimacing. Exhaling loudly, he makes another attempt.

Mary,

Where does the beginning end and the end begin? Was there ever a defining line between us? For, if there was, I am thankful it was a long, wide, gray span of momentary contentment with many blurred edges filled with love.

3

He lifts his head and stares off into an internal emptiness. Nick returns to his writing, not wanting to lose the thought.

You had such a grip on me, I forgot how to think, how to breathe. Somehow I always made it back to you when there was no air. I may have breathed in too deeply this time.

There was so much unspoken—covered up by the sheer intensity of us. Even now, I can feel the touch of your hands on my face, your tender lips brush against mine, the smell of your hair. I miss you, Mary, and hate that about me.

The words you last said left a hole be—

Nick drops the pen and takes the last slug of his drink. Looking down at what he's written, he's appalled by his own words because of what they reveal. Crumpling the paper into a ball, he tosses it into the corner, where it settles next to several others. That's enough for tonight. His heart has felt the right amount of pain—time to sleep—moments to forget.

Not so different, looking for answers . . .

Part 1

One

The past can haunt you.

His name: Nicholas James Pajak, forty-five, divorced, no children. His friends called him Nick. He was the majority owner of an established midsized detective agency located in the Old Town District of Las Vegas. His fifteen-year tenure as a police officer, and then detective, gave him the credibility required for the business. The company's main source of revenue was monitoring security systems and other specialty types of surveillance, including in-depth due diligence background checks for several of the larger casinos. On occasion, they picked up private cases involving allegations of spousal impropriety. Nick despised those cases, handing them off to his business partner, Giovanni "Joe" Papa. Joe was a Jersey mook who had relocated from the New York suburbs.

An ex-Manhattan cop with a heavy Jersey accent, he walked with a slight limp, favoring his left leg, thanks to the fragments of a thug's bullet still lodged there.

Their company, The Papa & Pajak Detective Agency, paid them both very handsomely. In spite of a listless economy, their business was booming, and they had added eighteen employees to the payroll in the past four years. Joe figured, "When times are tough, there's always one sector of the population willing to roll the dice and risk it all. That's Vegas. You gotta love it."

Nick's personal life, on the other hand, was strikingly different than his business life. Perhaps it was the divorce or the dumping himself into the job afterward—whichever, the ravages of time had taken their toll on him. Deep lines creased his forehead and crow's feet and premature graying provided a not-so-subtle hint of his turbulent past. At six foot three and weighing no more than a hundred and ninety pounds, Nick was slim to the point of being gangling. Apart from his height, he was average looking, with light brown eyes; he wouldn't stand out in most crowds.

When the divorce from Stephanie became final, he sold the place *they* had once called home and handed over the daily running of the business to Joe. He stayed on as silent partner, collecting a generous monthly dividend.

Nick sent his ex-wife a good chunk of the profits, far more than what he owed under the terms of the divorce, though he knew she would run through the money as if it were water through a colander. It took some time, but when the dust settled, the changes pointed him to another path. He accepted that he had to leave Las Vegas—too much of the past. There was nothing left for him there.

Nick landed in the city of Orange, the heartland of Orange County, California. This was where he had spent his youth, until his parents themselves divorced when he was seventeen. That was when Momma Pajak packed up the kids—Nick and his two sisters, Shannon and Pam—and headed to Las Vegas for a new life. Now, less than a block from his old childhood home off Harwood Street, Nick felt the irony of how life had turned out. He surmised that everyone returns home—eventually.

* * * * * *

"HEY, PAJAK, WHAT are you doing? Get your ass out there and mow section A23," snapped Jessup, the park's superintendent and boss man.

"Yes, sir. I was about—"

"I don't care what you were doing. *Ivamos, la hierba no se vacortor sola!*" barked Jessup in the best bastardized junior college Spanish money could buy.

Nick stood and placed both hands on his hips. Towering over the smaller man, he gave Jessup a look that suggested he should reconsider how to address him. It worked flawlessly.

"Sorry, Nick, I'm under a little stress today," Jessup said, and then looked out the door. "Miguel's not in today, so you have to work it alone. You should probably get started soon."

"I'm on it," Nick responded, pleased with Jessup's apparent attitude adjustment and gave him a nod. Nick left, leaving several of his fellow employees relaxing in what they referred to as the "lounge"—actually a storage shed with an aging tin roof. Overgrown bushes shielded the otherwise celebrated break area from the public.

Although he didn't need the money, Nick had taken a gardener job as a part-time employee at the seventy-three-acre Fairhaven Memorial Park and Mortuary, as a way to keep his mind occupied. The cemetery was a short drive from his place. Nick had always liked the sun on his face and took pride in fulfilling the physical demands of the position—it was exactly what he needed. But the biggest benefit was the complete lack of responsibility. There were no more employees to direct, no one to motivate, no papers to push or headaches over the bottom line. After a workday, all he had to do was go home, pour himself a drink, put his feet up, and unwind.

Nick rounded the corner and hopped onto what he considered *his* mower. It was an older Exmark, an outdated one-seater whose paint had faded to a dull shade of red. Gray primer showed through in the places where it had been heavily scratched. While his coworkers would have loved to be riding the latest, fanciest John Deere model, Nick was happy with the mower he called his *gal.*

As he motored down the cemetery's main road, he admired the abundance of flowers. During the holiday seasons, and especially Easter week, the park was filled with the pungent, sweet smell of roses and lilies. Nick understood why people came to visit their loved ones, leaving tokens of their missing. The bountiful displays of colorful bouquets warmed his heart. Before, Nick had been more of a shoot-first-and-ask-for-forgiveness-later type. His change of location and vocation had erased some of those old traits . . . or perhaps just buried them deeper. Either way, armed with a different perspective, he was literally willing to stop and smell the roses. He popped the mower up and over the curb and turned the key, shutting off the motor. It coughed and died.

Every Wednesday morning, apart from holiday weeks, the grounds were cleared of the previous week's flowers, ornaments, and other assorted items before being mowed. Since most of the graves had flat markers rather than vertical headstones, cutting the grass was made fairly easy. Management frowned on mowing over anything other than the grass. During his short time at the job, Nick had found a number of odd items left behind: fresh cigars, unopened beer bottles, polished heart-shaped rocks, an anchor, and once, a joint—tightly rolled and ready to smoke. Generally, everything got trashed. However, for a few of the longtime guys back at the lounge, the rule didn't apply to them, especially when it came to the smokables. They also kept a collection of the more bizarre trinkets stored on a hidden shelf in the rear of the lounge.

With a black trash bag in hand, Nick bent to pick up a wilting spray of tulips, stuffed them into the bag, and moved on to the next marker. He grabbed some dying roses out of an in-ground vase, dumped the remaining water, and replaced the vase bottom side up, all in one smooth motion. He advanced from one marker to the next, until the section appeared cleared. He took a quick look around to ensure there was nothing he would run over with the mower. Out of the corner of his eye, he caught a quick flash of light. He narrowed his eyes, trying to catch the flash again.

He dropped the trash bag and walked in the direction of the source. It seemed to be coming from an area mostly free of markers, a good thirty feet away. Reaching the approximate spot, he turned his attention to the lone grave in the sector. The marker was made of solid black marble, conventional, industry-standard 16 x 28 inches. There was nothing elaborate or opulent about the cut. Without reading the stone, he could tell it had been there for some time. A fine white calcium film lined the etched letters and numbers, likely caused by hard water deposits from the regular watering. In the upper left-hand corner was an engraving of a sleeping cherub; just below it lay a gold ring. Nick didn't pick it up but instead, moved closer to read the marker.

OPAL LYNN KRAFT
1960–1999

OUR BELOVED MOTHER, WIFE, DAUGHTER,

SISTER, GRANDCHILD, TEACHER,

FRIEND AND ANGEL.

"God . . . You were so young—and a mother," he muttered to himself. It took him to his days in the department, where he had investigated too many needless deaths. Sadness filled his heart. He knew better than to read the markers. They had warned him about that when he first took the job.

He rubbed the dirt off his fingers and crouched down to pick up the ring. It looked shiny and new. His detective instincts kicked in. He scanned the surrounding area and quickly came up with two plausible theories of how it had come to be there. The ring could have been dropped accidentally, from right where he stood. It could easily have fallen out of a pocket or purse, hit the surrounding grass and bounced onto the marker. But there was a problem with that theory. If the ring had somehow been clumsily mishandled, the odds of it coming to rest below the cherub and not in one of the many etched lines or grooved channels was highly improbable. Not to mention the "clink" sound it would have made hitting the marble.

Or, perhaps, the ring had been placed there deliberately. But who would have left what appeared to be a gold ring lying around for anyone to take?

He slipped the ring into his pocket, took note of the name on the marker, calculated the plot number, and went back to mowing the lawn.

By three thirty, when his shift ended, Nick was physically spent. Doing both his and Miguel's jobs had taken it out of him. However, the idea of doing a little investigative work gave him purpose for the day. His subconscious urged, nagged him, to do what he did best—solve mysteries. He had to find the owner of the ring. In a way, he missed his old job. Uncovering the truth, usually shrouded in some sort of deception, had always driven him. And now, this gold ring provided the perfect opportunity to touch the past and make things right—for someone.

Based on its small size, it's a woman's ring, he thought. *And if her husband dropped it there accidentally, he's probably going crazy looking for it.*

The pain of loss was something Nick knew firsthand.

He also ran through the possibility the ring had been left there intentionally. In that case, returning it could get dicey, definitely awkward, if not confrontational. Even so, Nick didn't subscribe to the school of thought that "no good deed goes unpunished," and was willing to risk it. He had to do what was morally correct for him—something in the business world he couldn't always afford to do.

Nick brushed the remnants of lawn clippings from his uniform and walked up to the park's main office.

"Hello, Miss Caroline," he greeted the receptionist at the front desk.

"Good afternoon, Mr. Pajak," she said peeking at her watch. "You're staying awfully late today, aren't you?" she asked, looking up.

Caroline was in her early seventies with silver hair, countless wrinkles, and coke-bottle glasses that gave her a unique look as if she were stuck in the 1950s. Nick found her endearing and forever welcoming. Whenever anyone walked through the front doors, regardless of their circumstances, she met them with a pleasant smile and a caring word.

"A bit," he said, resting his hands on the countertop.

"You so seldom come in here anymore." Her focus didn't waver from his eyes. "What is it that I can help you with today?"

"Miss Caroline, I was hoping you would say that." Nick paused. "I do have a favor I need of you." He smiled.

"Well. Let's see. What kind of favor?"

Nick leaned forward and lowered his voice, "How about the admin file for one of the plots?" He reached into his jeans pocket for the scrap of paper.

"Lawn section A23, last name Kraft, like the food company. The space number is 280G, if I did the math right." He smiled again.

She couldn't resist his smile, especially the way it curled up slightly higher on the left. "Fine, Mr. Pajak, I'll check for you this one time, but you know the park's policy. And I don't want to know anything about what you're up to."

She stood, threw him a quick look, and exited into the back room.

Caroline returned carrying a three-by-five index card, which she handed to Nick. He took a look at the card and gave Caroline a disappointed sneer.

"Sorry, Nick, Susan's in her office. This is the best I can do for now."

Susan, the park's records manager, took her job seriously and wouldn't have approved of an employee meddling in a customer's private affairs.

"Thank you. I understand." Nick's eyes twinkled.

"Now get out of here. And you're welcome," she said, shooing him out of the office. "I'll get the rest for you tomorrow."

Nick nodded and left.

Trusting your intuition.

Two

Nick rented an older home, single-story, typical early 1960s California ranch style. The roofline was low by today's standards, and included a wide overhanging eave that encircled the entire house. It had three small bedrooms and an open living room featuring a not-so-high vaulted ceiling and exposed beams. The kitchen had recently been upgraded with new granite counters and rubbed cherrywood cabinets nestled between the stainless steel Viking refrigerator and dishwasher.

The front yard had been professionally landscaped, with red and white roses lining both sides of the property. The expansive concrete driveway turned to the right, at a ninety-degree angle, leading to the attached two-car garage. The front entrance was ordinary, with the exception of the overhang that extended well beyond the eaves, sheltering the coir fiber welcome mat. The salmon-colored stucco and wood shake roof betrayed the house's age, in spite of its "Home and Garden" appeal.

The gardeners and maid came once a week; luxuries Nick could well afford. The less he had to do around the house, the better. What he liked about being a renter was when anything went wrong, he simply called the owners or went next door and knocked on their door.

His landlords, the Plowmans, responded quickly whenever Nick made a request. Michael and Melinda liked Nick, not only because he paid the rent on time and kept the house in pristine condition, but because they also considered him a friend. With their son off to college, they tended to keep to themselves. So their friendship with Nick was special. Michael believed Nick to be plainspoken and humble—real. Melinda had once said, "Nick, you have the eyes of a priest, sincere, confident, and yet, a little sad." Of course, being next door conferred certain advantages unavailable to absentee owners—they could check on him any time they chose.

Nick didn't mind their unannounced visits, although, most often, it was Michael who dropped by for a friendly word. Michael was a retired professor who had worked at UC Irvine. He had run a lab researching a cure for AIDS. Melinda headed up the real estate department for a local Bank of America in Orange. The Plowmans appeared to be happy sharing in each other's lives.

* * * * * *

ARRIVING HOME, NICK grabbed a water bottle out of the garage fridge and stripped down to his boxers and T-shirt. He would never track the day's dirt into the house. As soon as he was inside, he beelined it to his favorite piece of furniture, the leather recliner. It was old, scratched, and owing to its many years of use, the seat conformed perfectly to his butt. The recliner was the only surviving item from his old life and something he couldn't part with. To the right of the chair was an octagonal oak table, and on top of it, an antique Tiffany lamp he bought in Old Towne Orange. On the table Nick placed the water bottle, index card he had procured from Caroline, and the ring. Once ensconced in his old friend, Nick rolled back and stared up at the ceiling. The day had worn on him. He exhaled forcefully.

He reached over to turn on the light, then groped blindly for the ring. Finding it, he held it up to the last remnants of an evening sun streaming through the back window. He admired its luster. The ring itself was modest, as gold bands go, until he looked closer. With the hem of his T-shirt, he carefully polished the ring. On its outside surface was an inscription. In cursive script, the phrase "*Tomorrow I'll love you even more*" was engraved. He narrowed his eyes and slapped the ring down on the side table with such force it left a Nike logo-shaped ding.

Loving like that—so innocently—so wholly—was something he himself had once believed in. Now a reformed romantic, the idea of falling and staying in love was nothing more to him than a myth, like Santa Claus or the Easter Bunny. Sure, it always starts out with the best of intentions, trust, and great hope. But, eventually life turns those childish thoughts into unrecognizable feelings, misguided faith, and finally, with her walking out the door.

His stomach churned, his mind went to that place of unresolved anger—Stephanie, their past. He had dreamed they would dance forever. It had been over two years since that dreaded day. She left him on a Tuesday morning with a short note that read, "*I will forever love you, but I have more to give. I need to find my own way.*"

On her way out the door, she had appropriated every stitch of her clothing, including the tens of thousand dollars' worth of shoes. All that had remained were a few framed pictures representing some of their better times. He'd heard through the grapevine that she had justified her actions by saying, "Sometimes, love alone isn't enough." He never did understand that.

He shook his head trying to rid himself of the hurt. He looked over at the ring, not wanting to touch it. The ring symbolized a part of him that was no longer possible. And moreover, its dedication weighed on him as if the world was trying to tell him something—something bigger—something he had forgotten and needed to relearn. He didn't want to hear it. Anything dealing with Stephanie, love, and whatever the ring's inscription meant, he wasn't ready. For a brief instant he thought of throwing away the ring.

Reality settled his anger. Nick sipped from his water bottle and picked up the index card. Caroline's handwriting was neat and legible. There were two lines of information: the first, the owners' names and relationship to the deceased: Stu and Fran Milton—Parents. And on the second line, what appeared to be their home phone number.

He was bemused that the cemetery's plot had been purchased by her parents, considering her age. Usually one could safely assume that the deceased's spouse would have paid for the plot. However, not knowing the family dynamics, today's blended families, and the high divorce rate among a thousand other reasons, he could not say why her parents had stepped up. In any case, Nick didn't think it should pose a problem.

He went into the kitchen and picked up his cell. Taking a seat at the table, he tapped in the number, his adrenaline beginning to pump.

It rang once, then twice.

"Hello?" a woman's voice answered.

"Yes, I'm calling for a Mr. or Mrs. Milton," Nick said.

"Who's calling?"

"Ah . . . my name is Nick Pajak. And I work over at the Fairhaven Memorial Cemetery."

"Uh-huh."

"First, is this Mrs. Milton?"

"Yes, this is she. Go on."

"And you are the owner of the Kraft plot? Correct?"

"For God's sake, if you mean Opal, my daughter, yes."

"I believe I may have found something that belongs to you."

Silence.

"Speak up. What is it that you've found?" she said.

Nick paused, already tense at the curtness of her responses.

"Well, ma'am, this morning I found a ring lying on your daughter's marker. And I wanted to return it."

"I'm sorry, sir. But, I have no idea what you're talking about. A ring? It's not ours." Her voice rose.

Nick pressed on, wanting it to be theirs. "It's a gold band, ma'am. Perhaps your husband lost it. The outside of the band has an engraving on it. It says, '*Tomorrow*—'"

"Who is this again?" she cut Nick off.

"Ma'am, my name is Nick Paj—"

"Listen, I don't know you and don't really care what you want. But you can tell *him* that if he wants any information from me, he can call me directly. Better yet, advise your friend to leave us alone altogether."

"Tell who?" asked Nick.

"Oh, don't play coy with me, son. Tell Kent to move on. My little angel is in heaven. And—"

"Ma'am, I assure you I don't know any . . . Hello? Ma'am? Mrs. Milton . . . Hello?"

She had hung up.

Now that's interesting, he thought, *how the mere mention of the ring set her off. And who is this Kent guy? The husband? An ex? Now, that might explain why the parents had bought the plot. Still, I wonder about his side. There are always two sides.*

Nick was further drawn into the story behind the ring.

A voice echoed, "Don't let me go."

Three

Life according to Mary: Threshold.

The *Legacy* book: Pages 54–57

"Stay put and stick your head back into your book. I'll be back in a minute," the old man grumbled.

He got out of the '65 white Ford Ranchero, slammed the door shut, and walked over to another man. Moments earlier, Mary's grandfather had been breathing so heavily, the car's windows had fogged over, leaving her now with only a silhouetted view of the two men as they came together. She heard an angry exchange of words but couldn't make out what they were saying. She wiped away a patch of mist from the windshield and peered through the cleared streaks, wondering why they had come here in the first place.

Last night, Grandpa Heil had said, "We'll be going on a field trip tomorrow. It's a long one, so ya better get to bed early."

And they had been in the car all day, which, for a seven-year-old, felt like forever. Their only stop since leaving San Diego had been at a doughnut shop somewhere in the Los Angeles area. Mary could barely make out the wooden planks of a small pier through the driver's-side window. There was the sharp smell of salt in the air, though she had no idea where she was.

Then there was a loud bang. The sound echoed.

Mary saw the other man fall backward and then sit motionless on the ground. Her grandfather rushed back to the car.

"Okay, princess, time to go," he said, as he jumped in and started the car in one swift motion. They drove off.

"Who was that man you were talking to, Grampa?" Mary asked.

"No one," he replied sharply, breathing heavily again.

"What was that loud noise?" asked Mary. "You did hear it, didn't you?"

"Yeah. It was one of those pallets falling off the top of the heap of crates back there."

"Oh . . . What's a pallet?"

He didn't answer.

Mary gazed down at her book for a moment, and then back at her grandfather. "The man you were talking to, he fell down. Is he okay?"

"He's fine. He didn't feel too good and took a seat. He wanted me to leave just the same. Forget about it, princess. Okay?"

"Sure thing, Grampa."

On their way back to San Diego they stopped for gas. When Grandpa Heil got out to pump gas, Mary noticed he seemed to be moving faster than his usual relaxed pace, as if he was late for an appointment. Closing her eyes, tired from the long drive, she lay her head down on his coat. Feeling something hard against her cheek, she rearranged the folds of the coat. Then she slumped down against the fabric again. But, she could still feel the lump and pushed her hand in among the creases to find out what it was.

Smelling of fire, it was a pistol.

Four

Throughout the next morning's shift, Nick checked his watch hourly. He worked diligently, wishing time would hurry up and get to the day's end. His detective juice flowed, and he was surprised to find himself wanting the hunt and discovery. Unable to wait any longer, on his morning break, he headed straight for the main office and Caroline. Almost as if she had been expecting him, she handed over a manila folder saying, "Nick, I need to have it back tomorrow."

Nick said nothing, offering only a crooked smile, noting the seriousness of her tone. She acknowledged him with a grin of her own.

Knowing his break was already over, he rummaged through the file while walking out the door. Nothing immediately popped out to him. Leaving the file in his car, he ran back to the lounge to check back in.

* * * * * *

AT HOME, HE shuffled through the folder's contents.

"Where are you? Ah . . ." he beamed.

Nick pulled out a light pink sheet adorned with an elaborate blue frame border—Opal's official Certificate of Death. His eyes were drawn to the lower right corner and the official seal of the County Clerk Recorder of Orange County, California. In the middle of the page was the Spouse and Parent Information section.

"What the hell?"

The spouse's name was not Kent, but a Mack Kraft.

"Then who's Kent?" he mumbled to himself. The deeper he delved, the more doors appeared out of nowhere.

Nick scoured the folder for anything that referenced a Kent. Then, on the very last page, he found it—a receipt issued to a Kent Huffman.

It was stuck to the previous page with what appeared to be some kind of red juice. He peeled the two pieces apart. The receipt was a yellow duplicate for the purchase of a brass flower insert vase for $62.25. Stamped across it in large bold red lettering was the word "SERVICED" with a handwritten date of September 18th, no year. At the bottom, included in the Customer Order Information section, appeared the name Kent Huffman, signed, and, unbelievably, a telephone number.

Luck always requires an action, he thought.

Nick impulsively grabbed the phone and dialed the number. As he had so often done in the past, he relied on his intuition to provide for opportunity.

God, I've missed this.

The phone rang.

"Hello," a sweet-sounding woman answered.

"Is Mr. Huffman home?" Nick inquired.

"I'm sorry; he's out at the moment. Can I take a message for you?" Her reply seemed even more softhearted.

"Actually, no, ma'am. I need to speak with him personally. When do you think he'll return?"

"Not until later. But, please don't call me ma'am. I'm not that old."

Nick hesitated. *Okay?* "Might there be a better time tonight?"

"It could be a while. He and Angie are out celebrating their anniversary."

Hmmm, married.

"And then, you are?" Nick asked.

"I'm his sister, Mary Berean," she replied happily. "And you?"

"Well, good evening, Mrs. Berean."

"Oh no, it's miss. And who are you again?"

Nick chuckled to himself, liking her tenacity.

"My name is Nicholas Pajak." He paused, out of character, not sure where he was going with the conversation.

"And how can I assist you, Mr. Pajak?"

"Ah . . . It's possible I may be in possession of something that belongs to Mr. Huffman, and I would like to return it to him."

"And what exactly is it, Mr. Pajak?"

"Really, miss, I think it's best if I speak to him directly."

The line went silent for a moment.

Then in the sweetest tone, "Oh, Mr. Pajak, you can tell me."

Beguiling as her voice was, Nick resisted her appeal. "Please, miss, call me Nick."

"All right then, Mr. Nick," she responded, as if accustomed to the game. "So you know, I handle all sorts of matters for my brother, including business, and especially his personal affairs. Please don't be afraid to confide in me. I give you full permission. So, whatever you think you may have of his . . . I assure you, I can handle it for him."

Silence. Nick wasn't about to disclose anything else. He had already said too much. Considering the reaction from Opal's mother, discussing the ring or where he had found it was out of the question. There was no way he was going to make the same mistake twice. He took a moment, formulating a noncommittal response, but wanting to hear more of her lovely voice. She intrigued him.

"Listen, I can tell you're a good man," Mary continued, "and how wonderful of you wanting to return whatever it is to my brother. But, honestly, Mr. Nick, you can put your trust in me. Okay, how about this . . ." her voice suddenly wavered. "Why don't we meet? I'll bring Kent, and you can give whatever you have directly to him. I have his schedule right in front of me."

"Or, how about I meet him at his home? Maybe this Friday?" Nick interjected.

"Oh no, that won't do. He's an extremely private person and doesn't like people he doesn't know at his home. I hope you understand."

Nick's eyes narrowed, his eyebrows met as his forehead creased.

Who does this guy think he is?

"How about we meet tomorrow for lunch? He's free. Your choice. After all, you should be rewarded for your honesty."

Nick felt strange. Usually he was the one in control, calling all the shots. And now this Mary woman, with her enticing, sultry voice, seemed to have run him over.

"No need for that, miss," Nick said, hiding his curiosity.

"My, aren't you adorable, but no, dear. How about noon tomorrow at the Rutabegorz near the Orange circle? Do you know where it is?"

"Yes, but—"

"Great, then. We'll see you at noon tomorrow at Rutabegorz."

She abruptly hung up, leaving Nick to his own thoughts—uneasy and yet somewhat charmed by this odd woman.

It never worked like this at the agency. And what exactly is a Rutabegorz, he wondered.

Cracks in the ceiling.

Five

In satisfying his natural inquisitiveness, Nick discovered that Rutabegorz was one of those health-conscious restaurants which publicized serving some of the freshest organic fruits and vegetables in all of Orange County. Originally built in 1915 as a family home for an early citrus rancher, the Rutabegorz Orange location followed the company's tradition of being housed in a historic building. Less than a half block from Chapman University, the restaurant was a local hangout for students. Parents regularly met their kids there for a wholesome lunch while soaking up the collegiate atmosphere.

Nick did a quick survey of the restaurant's front patio area. Since it was exclusively occupied by groups of students, he determined that Mary and Kent had to be inside.

Noontime and the restaurant was packed. He used the main entrance, keeping his eyes open for two people who might be brother and sister.

A hostess approached him, "How many in your party?"

"Three. Do you mind if I take a look around to see if they're already here?"

"Sure, not at all, sir."

Nick took a few steps inside. There were a number of women with small children. Straight-ahead, the only two men in the restaurant were sitting together. In the far right corner, he noticed a woman sitting alone, and she was openly staring at him.

Wow, she's gorgeous. No, that can't be her. Maybe?

He had pictured Mary as unattractive, very possibly ugly, with black-haired arms and a matching mustache to boot. He wasn't sure how he had formulated this image of her. There were plenty of sweet-voiced, pushy, yet pretty OC ladies around.

Sure . . . I may as well.

He approached the woman. "Excuse me, miss, by any chance are you Mary?"

"Why, yes, I am Mary. Mr. Nick? I thought that might be you."

Mary stood up and hugged him as if being reunited with a long-lost friend. Nick towered over the petite woman. He returned the embrace hesitantly, caught off guard by her show of affection. When he pulled back he caught the slightest scent of coconut from her hair.

Damn, and you smell great too, he thought.

"I hope you haven't been waiting long," Nick said. "I had a few things to finish up. That's why I'm a little late. I apologize."

"Where's Mr. Huffman?" he asked, although he was thinking that a few moments alone with her might not be so bad.

Mary sat down. Her eyes darted around, and then rested squarely on Nick.

"Please sit. . . . Sorry, bad news, dear. Kent was called away this morning on some pressing business. He does send his regrets, and, if necessary, I can call him."

Still hovering over the table, Nick said hollowly, "Ah . . . then I should probably go. Perhaps a raincheck for another day?"

"Oh no, Mr. Nick, stay right here," Mary insisted. "Sit and have lunch with me. I don't get out and about in this part of town and . . . besides, you're here already." She smiled flirtatiously.

Is this the same woman I spoke with last night?

Nick sat down opposite her, avoiding eye contact, pretending to be unfazed by Kent's absence.

Perhaps I misjudged her. She's not bossy, just confident, friendly, he thought. Funny how men are so easily swayed by an attractive woman.

"Please, call me Nick. No need for any formality, I'm not that kind of guy."

Nick had yet to look at her directly. From afar, her appearance was intimidating, and up close, he didn't risk looking directly at her for fear of staring. He picked up the menu.

"Wonderful. Then, Nick, enlighten me. Tell me about yourself."

He could feel her eyes sizing him up. He believed his insecurity would soon come bubbling to the surface to be read by all. Luckily, the waitress appeared. Nick looked up, relieved at the distraction. Her name tag read Michelle.

"What can I get you two to drink?" waitress Michelle asked.

Mary spoke up, "Iced tea for me . . . Nick?"

"A water, thanks."

"That's an iced tea and a water. I'll be back in minute to take your order." She left.

"Well, continue, Nick. You were about to say . . .?" Mary intertwined her fingers on the table.

Nervously shifting in his chair, Nick decided he was too old to worry about some woman's opinion of him, regardless of how pretty she was. He stared directly into Mary's eyes. All at once, he was taken in, instantly mesmerized. It was like staring at the sun, knowing you shouldn't, but unable to look away. Mary's eyes were a dazzling shade of light hazel. Her features were those of a classic beauty: large round eyes, full lips, and a small nose and chin. She had olive skin, which made her eyes appear ever increasingly luminous. Her face was framed by long, slightly wavy auburn hair, with highlighted strands throughout. The lack of wrinkles confused him as to her age—maybe late thirties, early forties, he guessed—and that was solely based on the initial stages of crow's feet visible when she smiled. Nick thought she was probably the most beautiful woman he had ever met in person. *She has to be a model.*

"Not much to say. Just a normal guy." He broke eye contact.

"Meaning what?"

"Nothing, really."

"Oh . . . I see. You're one of those big, strong, silent types."

Nick chuckled, finally cracking a smile. "Yeah, kinda like that."

Mary reached across the table and patted Nick's arm in mock sympathy. As she pulled her hand back, she knocked over the flower vase between them. She quickly righted it, spilling only an ounce or two of water.

Nick laughed, throwing his napkin on top of the puddle.

"It wasn't that funny." Mary's cheeks reddened, and then she giggled. "Okay, maybe a little. Well, Mr. Strong-Silent-Man, what do you do for a living?"

Nick thought for a moment, and then replied, "I pretty much pick up dead flowers and cut a little grass."

Mary laughed halfheartedly, convinced he was joking. "And how long have you been doing that?"

"A short while, a few months."

"And . . .?"

"And . . .?"

"It's like you give me a potato chip while I'm dying of thirst out here in Death Valley. Are you always this way?"

Nick hated small talk. Worse, he hated talking about himself. He reached into his blazer's interior front pocket, pulled out the gold ring, and placed it on the table.

"This is what I found."

Mary glanced at the ring, then into Nick's eyes. He held her gaze for all of four seconds before looking away.

"There's no chitchat with you, is there? All business, huh?"

"Now, look at it closely," Nick persisted, intent on maintaining his focus. He didn't want to lose himself in her eyes.

"I can tell you right now, that is not my brother's." Reluctantly, Mary picked up the ring. "Look, Nick, I know you have good intentions and want to—"

Mary went silent. She dropped the ring, placed her hands over her mouth, and mumbled, "Oh no, it *is* his."

The mind is the real battlefield.

Six

The ring bounced twice, and then whirled in circular rotations until it spun itself out, coming to rest next to Nick's thrown napkin.

The situation reminded him of the day his wife left, at least the being blindsided part. His plan had not been to shock Mary—he wanted her to shut up—she dabbled on a nerve too long. The lack of self-control confirmed he had lost the *edge* that once made him an elite detective. Thinking back, he realized his restraint drain had begun with Stephanie's "Dear John" letter. He handled her leaving badly. Only after several hundred dollars' worth of drywall repairs and replacement of a few broken picture frames was he remotely able to tolerate any thoughts of Stephanie or their past life together.

Nick eyed Mary, waiting for her next reaction. How would she handle this information?

Mary's expression went from surprise to anger.

"How could he do this to Angie?" Her voice became loud. Her shoulders tightened in apparent disgust, her fingers fidgeted, twisting her napkin into never-ending loops.

Nick leaned forward.

"Mary, judging by your reaction, the ring's a problem for you. Take a moment and breathe; relax."

"What an asshole."

"Excuse me?"

"My brother's such an asshole."

"Whoa. Slow it down a bit before you start saying something you might regret." Nick swallowed. "Let me fill you in on the details—"

"How could he have done this to Angie? She's about the nicest woman in—"

"Stop! Please. I found the ring in a cemetery."

"What?" She instantly put the brakes on whatever emotional roller coaster she was on. "Cemetery? Oh really."

Mary's neck turned red.

"Yeah, I found it on a grave marker."

"Huh . . . no. What? Wait. Are you trying to pull some kind of a scam? Because if you are, it's not going to work on me, buster." Confusion spread across her face. "Why would you say—"

"Okay, enough with the accusations." Nick paused. "Can you just not say anything until I'm finished? Okay?"

Mary's mouth dropped open, and then closed in astonishment as if she had never been spoken to like that. Her lips tightened, forming lines around her mouth like a picket fence that suggested she might be older than he had thought. She nodded, though clearly seething.

"Thank you. As I was trying to say," Nick collected himself, "I'll give you the nickel version. I work over at the Fairhaven Memorial Park off Fairhaven Street. I discovered the ring lying on top of this woman's marker. After a little research, I followed a few leads, and believe it to be your brother's."

"Can I speak now?"

Already exhausted, Nick replied, "Sure, go ahead."

"Are you out of your mind? Come on, Nick, you believe it to be Kent's? How? And why? What—it's not like you're some kind of detective! And I'll bet—"

"Actually, Mary," Nick interrupted, "I used to be a detective, crime scene investigation unit, to be precise."

"Uh-huh . . . and I was born yesterday. Oh, better yet, I'm a world-famous actress and one-time mistress of the Prince of Wales." Mary's voice rose with each syllable, the redness spreading to her chest.

Ignoring her, Nick went on, "Here's the odd part. It was at the gravesite of a woman who died almost two decades ago. Now, based on where I found the ring, and having tied Kent's name through her administrative file, I believe with certainty that it is his. He could have intentionally placed it on the grave, or it could have simply fallen out of his pocket. I'm not sure—"

"Her name."

"Her name?" Nick repeated.

"What's the woman's name?"

"Opal Lynn Kraft."

"I don't know of any Opal Lynn whatever. Besides, Kent's been married for over twenty years."

"That doesn't mean the ring isn't his."

"Yeah, yeah, right," Mary replied, leaning back.

"Listen, Mary, I have no idea of the relationship between your brother and this Opal woman, but you said it yourself, the ring is his. Or are you now changing your mind?"

"No . . . yes . . . no. I don't know."

"Are you sure he's never mentioned an Opal to you before?"

Mary laid her hands flat on the table. Doubt crept into her voice. "No, I don't think so." After a short pause she continued, "But he does keep things to himself."

Nick had already begun to profile her brother in his mind.

Kent Huffman, a private man, is prone to keeping secrets— even from his own family, doesn't like outsiders in his home. Mary gives the impression he's something of a recluse—and missing today's meeting is an indicator.

There are two confirmed facts: Kent bought a vase insert for Opal's grave, and he's currently estranged from Opal's mother. Mary's initial reaction to the ring inscription further supports my case. Even more interesting is, what was Kent doing at the grave site in the first place?

An awkward silence fell between them. Nick moved back in his chair, crossing his arms. Hearing the crunch of paper against his forearms, he remembered the receipt. He pulled out a copy of the cemetery's work order and placed it in front of Mary.

"Is this your brother's signature?" Nick pointed, and then tapped on the entry.

Mary bent forward and looked at the signature. She shrugged her shoulders. "This doesn't prove anything."

"It establishes proof they knew each other. Why else would he have bought a vase insert for her?"

"Okay, maybe." Mary pushed the paper back toward Nick. "Were you really a detective?"

"Yes, ma'am."

Silence again.

"Fine. Nick, I don't want to play twenty questions with you anymore. Can you help me out and speak like a normal person to me? No more detective-lingo-type talk. Please?"

"Sorry. I thought I was doing pretty well."

Mary again reached out and lightly brushed the back of Nick's hand. "Of course, you did."

Her gentle touch turned into a light caress. Nick felt that in spite of her rather erratic behavior, Mary seemed to understand the sort of man he was.

All Nick could do was smile and enjoy her touch. It had been such a long time. He didn't return the gesture. He couldn't. The heart beats only when you're alive, and Nick was sure his had been strangled and bled out years ago.

* * * * * *

THEY ORDERED LUNCH and the conversation turned to things of a personal nature. Nick spoke briefly of moving to California, his business partner Joe, and their detective agency. Mary mentioned her grandmama Matos and the influence she had had on her life. How she hated the color yellow on anything. She also touched on the failure of her own first marriage and working for her brother Kent. None of their conversation went much beyond the surface. Mary gave every sign of being interested in Nick, from hair flipping to the assertive touching of his hand and arm any time he said anything vaguely funny. Nick, intelligent as he was, didn't recognize genuine flirtation when it was showered upon him, though he did notice her hand trembled a little whenever she reached for him.

Nick paid for lunch over Mary's objections. Mary returned the ring to Nick, saying she wanted to do a little investigation of her own before approaching her brother. They exchanged cell phone numbers with assurances of being in touch—soon.

Surprises of today . . . hope for tomorrows.

Seven

Life according to Mary: Understanding a different truth.

THE *LEGACY* BOOK: Pages 58–62

"Grandmama, I had another of those dreams last night," Mary said. Her shoulders drooped in disgust at failure to somehow control her own subconscious. Her eyes were filled with sleep and sadness. She rubbed them sluggishly.

"Come over here, baby, and seet," her grandmother said in a heavy Portuguese accent. She patted the seat next to her.

At eighty-four, Grandmama Matos was the matriarch on Mary's father's side of the family, and when she spoke, everyone listened. A Brazilian immigrant, she had come to America with only ninety-eight dollars and three dresses to her name. Even then, at the ripe age of nineteen, her magnetic personality in combination with her exotic beauty commanded attention—especially from men. Having been married twice, outliving both husbands, her view of the world had remained unaltered. She had never accepted the ways of what she referred to as "this generation of spoiled children," and "women who act as men." Strong and single-minded, she held an uncompromising belief in God and the supernatural.

Mary took the seat next to her and lightly touched her hand.

"Tells me, dears, what this about?" asked the old woman.

"Grandmama . . . it's the dreams. I don't like them. They're really scary, and when I wake up I'm supercold. I wish they would go away."

Grandmama Matos squeezed Mary's hand for reassurance, although her face told another story. "What happens this one?"

Mary understood what she meant. "Remember last week when Grampa Heil took me on that trip? I saw a man fall down after speaking with Grampa. It was him in my dream."

"Aha." She looked away from Mary.

"Or I think it was about that man. He had the same body, but his face turned all black . . . I mean, like I couldn't see his eyes or nose. They were gone, sorta like they were missing, and instead, I saw only black outlined space. He had his hair and stuff, just everything was black."

"Goes on."

"Anyways, I saw that man in a hospital room. He was sick or something . . . tubes were coming out of his arms and mouth. That's when his face went black. A nurse came over and pulled the bedsheet over his head. She turned and looked mean at me. She told me to get out. She said I didn't belong there. That's when I woke up all cold and stuff." Mary's head dropped again.

Grandmama Matos released her hand, then leaned back. She realized Mary had come across a truth the family didn't dare talk about. Finally, she spoke.

"*Mary, como? Voce tem oito anos agora.*"

"Oh, Grandmama, I'm almost eight. I think that's what you asked? Could you talk in English? It's easier for me," Mary said.

"I try." She tapped Mary's leg twice and continued. "It times I should tell you. I was praying that you not have those kind dreams. Now, I know."

"What? Those kind of dreams? Huh?" asked Mary, confused.

"*Sim*, those dreams. Not cause night last, but the lotta them you told me before. They're called *sonhos pretos.*"

Mary frowned, looking puzzled.

"En Englesh, dream dark. No—black dreams, that's it. Our *maldição de família.*" She leaned closer to Mary, covering her mouth, apparently surprised at her own lack of discretion.

"You're scaring me, Grandmama." She understood *maldição de família,* which meant family curse.

"It's okay, *meu* baby."

"No, really, Grandmama. Stop it," Mary said, covering her ears. "A curse? You're wrong. Please say you're wrong."

The grandmother pulled her close.

"No, baby, it was from long ago time. . . . You'd see evil's future. Anyone you dreams with black face, something very bad happen to them, maybe even to die."

Mary pulled away, gazing into Grandmama's eyes, wanting a different meaning from her words.

"Then, the man in the hospital bed . . . is he dead, for real?"

"*Sim*, yes."

"Help me, Grandmama. Please make it go away. I don't want this." Mary started to cry.

"*Meu* baby, is nothing can be done. I have tried. I live with that my whole life and never wish for you."

Grandmother Matos's eyes began to well up, understanding what was in store for her granddaughter. She turned her head away, so Mary couldn't see her tears.

Eight

The moment Nick got home he sat down at the kitchen table and started writing. He couldn't get Mary out of his mind. *What is this feeling?* A smile crossed his face.

Nick wrote:

I met someone today. She is not at all how I thought she would be, not that you can tell what someone is like over the phone. In spite of finding her to be moody and a bit offbeat in her behavior, I like her. Perhaps my perception has been influenced by her exceptional beauty. I wonder what that says about me.

Nick lifted the pen, pushed the hair off his forehead, and continued.

She has the softest hands I've ever felt. Her delicate touch got to me. I feel ashamed I didn't stand to say a proper good-bye to her.

I couldn't. My mind had been racing, envisioning the possibilities of her. It was a split-second cost-benefit decision. I imagined that if I stood, she might not notice at first, but if she were to hug me, there would be no mistaking my sail at half-mast.

I hope she didn't find me unsophisticated. Certainly, better to be considered ill-mannered than to reveal what I was actually thinking about.

I don't know why I'm always so hard on myself. She's a stunning beauty, and I'm sure this happens to her all the time. It's obvious she's one who doesn't lack for attention. Yes, she caught me staring several times, but each time graciously looked away. In between those moments, I stole additional glimpses of her lips— wondering . . . That's what got me into my predicament in the first place. I wanted to kiss her. Why didn't I?

What am I afraid of?

Nick put down the pen. Another question unanswered, another piece of paper for his drawer.

* * * * * *

LATER, HIS HEAD resting comfortably against the back of the leather chair, remote control in hand, he felt good about the day's events, except for the not standing part. She had been on his mind since leaving the restaurant. Though knowing little about her, he wanted to see her again. He wondered about her past. Everyone has baggage—something to hide. What was hers?

He marveled how the discovery of a plain gold ring had led to their meeting. And how her hair, with its intoxicating fragrance, had enchanted him. Some men prefer the verbena or lilac aroma concoctions from a fancy brand-name perfume. Not him—one whiff of her coconut essence and he was in trouble.

Nick had planned to wait the obligatory three days to call her—time enough to let her wonder if he was interested—but not so much time that she would feel rejected. The plan failed miserably, and he called her later that night. They talked until one in the morning.

They made a dinner date for the following Saturday.

She already held him with the slightest touch.

Nine

Saturday morning passed at a snail's pace as Nick anticipated *the date.* Around 1:00 p.m. and still in his boxers, he heard a knock at the front door.

"Be there in a minute," Nick yelled out on his way to the bedroom to throw on a pair of jeans.

"It's only me, Nick."

Nick recognized the voice of Michael, his landlord, and decided to answer the door as he was.

Michael, looking down at Nick's underwear, said, "I can see I caught you at a bad time." His face held a sense of unease.

"Not at all. Is there a problem?"

"Yeah. Do you have a couple of minutes? I could use some advice," Michael said.

"Sure. Can you hold on? I should probably put on a pair of pants. Don't want the neighborhood to start talking about us."

Michael snickered, squeezing out a brief smile.

"Hey, and while we're at it, I wanted to show you something inside the garage."

"Okay, great. I'll wait out here," Michael said while focusing on a couple of the paint patches curling up under the front door's eaves.

A minute later the garage door opened. Nick, now jeaned, stood next to his car holding two opened beers.

Nick handed Michael a bottle. "You look like you could use one."

"Thanks. It's been a morning I'd like to forget." Michael took a long gulp and started right in. "You know some of the problems we've had with our son. Well, his latest is a real doozy." He took another swig. "And with you being an ex-cop and all, thought you could give me some guidance."

Nicked nodded. "If I can."

"Last night, Adam went to a party near the college. You know, college kids and beer." Michael looked at his own beer, "Okay, old guys and beer too," he chuckled.

"Anyway, he had a beer there, and he swears it was only one. Then after a few minutes he decided to leave. Two other of his friends asked if they could bum a ride home. And Adam being the good guy said, 'No problem.' The second they pulled away from the curb he was red-lighted by the police.

"I'm sure the car's cab reeked of alcohol. Adam admitted to having a beer. So, the officer did the whole sobriety testing thing. He passed them all including the breathalyzer. I think he registered a .01. The problem is, he's two weeks shy of being twenty-one. He wasn't arrested. But the officer did take his driver's license away and gave him this ticket."

Michael handed Nick the ticket. Nick perused the written violation numbers and checked boxes. Then he took a sip of beer. "There's good and bad news."

Michael cringed. "I'm surprised there's any good news at all."

"For court purposes this isn't necessarily considered a DUI. This ticket is for an underage minor drinking while driving. There's a big difference. I'm sure he'll have to attend a few classes, pay a fine, etc. As long as he does what the court says, he should be okay.

"And the bad news . . . Adam can kiss his driver's license adios for a year. California DMV has this one-year mandatory license suspension rule regardless of what the courts say. Looks like he's got thirty days driving left before the suspension starts."

"That's it?" Michael looked confused.

"There're always a few exceptions, but based on what I've read about California law, I'd focus my energy on getting educated about the courts and try to appeal to them. You could spend a lot of time and money fighting the DMV in getting his license back."

Michael appeared somewhat relieved.

"I'll tell you what. When you get the court date, I'll go with you. Even hold your hand if you like."

"You'd do that for us?" Michael asked. "I'll probably take a pass on the holding hands. But . . . you never know."

Nick laughed and ironically offered him another beer. He didn't have the heart to show him the termite damage he found in the corner of the garage. Piling on bad news wasn't his style.

* * * * * *

THE DAY TURNED into an afternoon of several beers and a Lakers game with Michael. All the while, Nick kept one eye on the clock. His heart jumped a little as the minutes seemed to quicken. He didn't want to be rushed getting ready for her.

Nick had bought himself a tie, the first in many years, to mark the occasion and in hopes of more to come. He spent more than three hundred dollars on the Italian designer brand, Vitaliano Pancaldi, easily tripling the cost of any other he owned. He thought it made him look sharp and was sure to impress the lovely Mary.

As soon as the game ended, he pushed Michael out the door. Then he showered, shaved, put on his best suit, the new tie, and drove to Mary's.

"I'm still here," whispered in his ear.

Ten

Life according to Mary: Nefarious, another name for Mom.

THE *LEGACY* BOOK: Pages 75–76

"But, Mom, I love him," she said.

"You're only sixteen years old, young lady. How in the world do you think you're ready for this type of responsibility?"

"Buddy will get a job, and we'll be fine," Mary persisted.

"No. Absolutely not. *I'll* be the one who ends up taking care of it."

"Mom, that won't happen."

"Then answer me this: has Buddy *ever* had a job?"

"No, but—"

"Exactly. He knocks you up and can't even come over here and talk to me like a real man. What do you expect will happen once the baby's born?"

"I really hate you. . . . You've never given him a chance."

"Give him a chance? Listen up, missy, I wasn't the one who spread her legs wide open and got pregnant. And I'll be *damned* if I'll be the one to pay the price because you're a little slut."

"You don't understand. I love him!"

"Mary, you have no idea what love is, and it's certainly not about having a bastard kid. This discussion is closed. Not another word. I'll set it for next week and that's final."

And it was final.

The night before the procedure, Mary dreamt of a baby boy with an all-black face.

Eleven

Mary lived less than a mile away. Nick turned onto Adams Avenue and glanced at the notecard positioned on his lap for the exact address. As he drove through the old neighborhoods, familiarity came back to him in waves. He remembered his elementary school was just down around the corner where he played on the swings and had his first crush on a girl named Darlyn. How his sixth-grade teacher would pick his nose whenever he thought no one was watching. Pulling up to Mary's house, Nick peered through the passenger-side window, assessing her residence.

The property appeared well maintained. The house was a standard 1950s-era, single-story type, with large overhanging eaves that provided abundant shade year-round. The lawn was a lush green, and rows of roses and lavender lined both sides of the property. Three mature liquidambar trees dotted the front lawn, and the heavy odor of blooming star jasmine filled the air. Much like Nick's rental, the home had a nostalgic California charm.

Nick made his way up the pathway of reclaimed red bricks and onto the front porch.

He knocked and wiped wet palms on his pants. Peering through one of the six small windows in the mahogany door, he spotted Mary approaching. His tie felt like it was getting tighter.

Whoa, you are gorgeous, Nick thought. His neck muscles twitched.

Mary wore a silky black dress, no bra. Even for her age, her breasts appeared quite perky. Nick took great notice. The dress's plunging neckline and slit up the thigh accented her sensuous femininity. He had to force himself not to stare and averted his eyes momentarily. But the temptation was too great; his eyes seemed to move of their own accord, watching intently as she drew near.

When the door opened, Nick's eyes instantly refocused. As a man, he would love to have continued eyeballing the dress, how it clung to her body, accentuating her every ample curve. Already in over his head, he knew being crass wouldn't help his cause.

"Please come in, Nick. My, you do look handsome," Mary said with a confident smile, flashing her pearly whites.

Nick managed a meager "thank you" as he crossed the threshold. He immediately caught the aroma of something cooking.

Weren't we supposed to be going out to eat? Interesting, he thought.

The foyer broke off into three directions, each leading to a different section. To his right, the kitchen; to the left, presumably the bedrooms; and straight-ahead, an open area and the TV viewing room. Mary grabbed his hand and led him into the kitchen. She snuck a peek down at his sweating hand.

"Nick, instead of going out tonight, I decided to make us dinner. I hope you don't mind? I have so much to tell you. Please sit." Mary let go of his hand and pointed at a table on the other side of the kitchen.

"Okay." His tie felt like a noose as everything seemed to be moving too fast.

"I love to cook, but when it's only me here, well . . . you know."

Attempting to appear unfazed by the change of plans, Nick unbuttoned his jacket and took a seat at the glass-topped table. Cushioned in his chair, he watched discreetly as Mary moved around the kitchen. She glided from place to place, selecting a bottle from the wine rack, then moving to the counter to pluck a butterfly corkscrew from a drawer. With her hands full, she closed the drawer with her hip, approached Nick, and set the bottle of pinot grigio and corkscrew on the table in front of him.

"Based on our conversation the other night, I thought you might like this wine. I know you're not a big wine drinker, but I picked it up hoping you'd try it."

She touched the top of Nick's left shoulder on her way back into the kitchen, saying, "It's on the sweeter side . . . like you."

"Uh, thanks. . . . You have a nice place here," Nick strained in an attempt at small talk. He held the bottle of wine between his legs, trying to pry out the cork.

Mary seemed to sense the unease in his voice. She turned quickly, causing her hair to fan out, elegant and uniform. She walked back over to Nick, leaned down until they were face-to-face, and lightly kissed him on the cheek. She whispered, "Nick, I'm glad you're here. Please relax. I promise I won't bite . . . at least not tonight."

The bottle slipped down almost out of his hands. He caught it before it hit the floor.

Did she notice?

"Need a little help with that opener? It can be tricky." Mary smiled.

He had no idea how to handle this caliber of woman. *She is obviously out of my league,* he thought. Yet, there she was, right in front of him, saying all the right things. Would he make a move tonight? Could he touch her, kiss her? Oh, how he wanted to.

Nick wilted over his own indecision. "I should cancel our restaurant reservation," he said.

"Only if you think you can trust my cooking." Mary giggled her way back to the kitchen, clearly aware he was watching her every move. She deliberately exaggerated the sway of her hips.

"If you can cook as good as you look in that dress, I'm in for the meal of my life."

Mary looked back. "Oh, you like the dress?" She lifted an arm above her head, wrist limp, and thrust out her hip.

"Showoff," he murmured. A smile slowly spread across his face. He loosened his tie.

Mary turned back to the stove and checked on the two pans she had been cooking. The scented bouquet of simmering wine and mushrooms filled the room. Chicken Marsala and oven-roasted rosemary potatoes were on the night's menu. She grabbed two wineglasses from the shelf next to the refrigerator and sat down opposite Nick. "So, call," she said.

Nick, staring off into the air, had completely forgotten about the reservation. Mary looked at the wine bottle, still unopened. She smiled. She knew.

* * * * * *

AFTER CLEARING THE dishes, Mary dropped a large book onto the kitchen table. It was a hardback, all-black cover, with oversized yellow letters spelling out the word "Audion."

"What's this?" Nick asked.

"I took it from my brother's house. It's his high school yearbook," Mary smiled. "I've got something to show you."

"You stole his yearbook? Does he know?"

"Oh, Nicky, don't be such a worrywart. He'll get it back."

Nick chuckled, enjoying her nonchalant attitude. But he wasn't too keen about being called Nicky.

Sitting on the opposite side of the table, Mary opened the book, turned to the page she had marked with a Post-It note, and flipped it around so he could see it.

"Now, look at this," she said, pointing at some writing.

"Do you see it? It says Opal." Her voice rose with excitement.

"You're not the only one around here who can play detective," Mary giggled. "You got me thinking about my brother and that ring. So I went over to his house and did a little investigation of my own. While in his office, I came across his senior yearbook, actually his only yearbook. I don't know if I told you before, but back then, we didn't have much. Anyway, I looked for an Opal in the index and didn't find any. Flipping through the pages, almost as it was by fate, in the 'Reflections' section I found this paragraph written by him."

She tapped her finger on the paragraph.

Kent Huffman
To the Future: Football'4yrs2Track
4DebateteamFRML&dancesOpalLM
alwaysbepartofmylifeTILYEM-GTw
FriendsSCKAJJLBMBwLoveM@B

"I have no idea what the letters 'L' or 'M' stand for. But look, it says Opal!"

"I do," Nick replied without as much as a glance at the book. "First, explain to me what a reflections section is."

"Oh," Mary paused. "It's a section where seniors write something about themselves, times at school, sports, teachers—that sort of thing. So, the letters 'L' and 'M,' what do they mean?"

"Huh, interesting." Nick purposely avoided answering. "My high school didn't have anything like that. What a great idea."

"Nick, really."

"All right. . . . Her maiden name was Opal Lynn Milton. I got it from her death certificate. Now, there's the second connection between the two. Let me take a closer look at it."

Mary nudged the yearbook toward him.

Nick carefully read the passage, dissecting the meaning of each letter.

"Here." Nick started to turn the book back to Mary.

"No, that's okay. I want to sit next to you."

Mary rose, came around the table, pulled out the chair next to Nick, and scooted up close.

"Okay, go ahead." Mary was smiling ear to ear.

Nick continued, "It reads 'FRML&dancesOpalLMalway sbepartofmylife TILYEM.' The first part is easy, Formal and other dances, Opal Lynn Milton, you will always be part of my life. The 'TILYEM,' now that's fascinating."

Nick leaned back in his chair and thought.

"Hold on. It can't be that simple."

Nick reached into his back pocket and pulled out his wallet. Unfolding it, he searched through the bill compartment and pulled out the ring. He leaned forward, placing his elbow on the table, twiddling the ring between his fingers. Nick laughed and smiled broadly.

"What? Tell me." Mary playfully grabbed Nick's arm. "Tell me!"

"Mary, look."

"What?"

"It's the ring's inscription, 'Tomorrow I'll love you even more.' That's the 'TILYEM'; it's an acronym."

"No way. Wow, how beautiful." Mary smiled for reasons that seemed to go beyond reassurance that her brother was one of the good guys.

Then she began to tear up.

Tears are not exclusive to the lonely.

Twelve

Nick's quiet ways had served him well over the years. Whether inborn or learned, his silence had proven an invaluable tool. The ability to listen, to hear beyond one's own bias, was indeed a rare skill. Because of his career choice, the opportunity to hone the talent had been limitless. In his prime, he could detect a lie by the merest hesitation in a person's voice. Oftentimes, the slightest shift in facial expression or the blinking of an eye had doomed many a suspect's fate. What may have appeared an effortless deductive genius to some was, in fact, the result of many years of practice. He considered it a blessing. But, as with any blessing, there was a cost.

For Nick, the price had been enormous. His failure to maintain close personal friendships, apart from his business partner, Joe, was one. But the biggest, and most important, was the breakdown of his marriage to Stephanie.

He had pinned the blame on the infertility issue—after all, it was his fault. For reasons known only to God Himself, Nick was plagued with an extremely low sperm count. Initially, Stephanie said she had never wanted children. She often proclaimed the joys of being a DINK, "double income with no kids," and how she loved being with *only* her man. How could she ask for anything more?

Nick did try. He went on every known diet guaranteed to increase the number of his little swimmers. He ate oysters by the pound and rarely drank or smoked. He even doubled his tithing to the church and prayed for a miracle. Every month, after meticulously calculating the date of her ovulation, they would make love relentlessly. There were times she would frantically call him to come home in the middle of the workday. He would make up some lame excuse and rush home to be with her. Unfortunately, the hours she spent with her knees in the air after their lovemaking sessions proved fruitless.

Stephanie endured five failed in-vitro procedures, Nick by her side every step of the way. Ultimately coming to the realization that a child of their own wasn't in the cards, they tried adoption. Once again, life got the better of them. Both times, the birth parents changed their minds at the last moment and took their babies home. Exhausted and emotionally spent, Stephanie gave up the fight. She moved into her own apartment and soon shacked with up her boss, who came with a ready-made family—two children and a wife.

Nick died a little every time he learned more about her new life. His love for her faded away bit by bit. His heart, much like his sexual desire, withered. Finally, all that he had once trusted in became a thorn, causing a sharp pain every time he thought of her. Tears flowed heavily for the first nine months, in silence, as his soul turned. Each night he fell into cataclysmic nightmares of abandonment without resolution. He came to understand how a person could die of a broken heart.

Still, deep down, he concealed another, greater culpability of guilt. He never asked why, after all of their years together, did she suddenly want a child? Maybe he hadn't been there for her—with the right words, any words.

He was fed up with making the same mistakes. Since the divorce, he seemed to have fallen back into the same pattern—on all four dates—excluding Mary. At first, the women didn't mind his strong, silent manner. They might have even considered it charming. So Nick let them talk— he understood people loved to talk about themselves, and he had no problem providing them with a platform. Later, when they were all talked out and looking for a deeper engagement, Nick could only offer the occasional "Yeah" and a nod. He was empty . . . then.

* * * * * *

THEY MOVED TO the living room and sat on the couch. Mary edged closer, looking up longingly into Nick's eyes. Her smile was broad, conveying more than words.

Mary inched her mouth closer to his. Their lips touched, and in an instant, she was in Nick's lap. She ran her hands through his thick brown hair. Nick gently supported her lower back, drawing her ever closer. Abruptly, she pulled back, as if the moment was more than she had bargained for.

"I'm so sorry, Nick," she said, quickly slipping off his lap and turning away, staring at her knees, apparently overcome by shame.

"For what?"

"For kissing you first. I wasn't brought up that way."

"Don't be. I'm not." Nick grabbed her right hand. Her eyes remained downcast. "Look at you—you're perfect. The second I saw you in that dress tonight I wanted to . . ."

Mary glanced over and up into his eyes.

". . . hold you. Kiss you."

"Oh, Nick, you're so wrong. You don't understand. The things I'm already feeling for you. You scare me."

Mary looked down, pulling her hand away, and sat up rigid. Awkwardness fell between them.

Nick rubbed his chin. "And what exactly are you afraid of?"

"I can't. Not tonight," she muttered.

Mary immediately stood up, and without looking back, said, "Excuse me for a minute," and walked out of the room.

Nick shook his head. *What a strange night.*

WANTING TO QUENCH his dry mouth he went into the kitchen, poured himself a half glass of wine, strolled back to the couch, and waited. Patience had always been his friend.

When Mary returned, she walked directly up to Nick, crouched down before him, and sat back on her ankles. Her eyes had a touch of redness and the scent of a floral perfume trailed behind. Nick leaned forward, elbows on knees, chin in his hands.

Mary tilted forward onto her knees, extended her arms frontward, and rubbed the outsides of Nick's thighs. Not knowing what she would do next, Nick raised his arms and leaned back, unconfident about touching her. She lay her head on his lap. What was he to do? Ineptly, he returned her tender gesture by caressing her back. After several moments, Nick pulled her up by the shoulders and wrapped his arms around her. He drew her closer between his legs. His heart raced with the first touch of Mary's protruding nipples pressed against his shirt. A surge of excitement ran through his body. Any thoughts of her previous odd behavior quickly vanished.

"I'm sorry for being such a pill," Mary whispered into his ear.

Releasing his hold, Nick held her away from him, needing the separation. "Let me tell you a story about myself."

Mary arched backward and sat back on her ankles, hands lingering on his knees, all her attention on him.

"Wonderful, please do." She put on a smile, eyes still red.

"Great," Nick said.

He slipped down to the floor. Mary moved back, giving him room. Nick flopped one leg over the other in an attempt to sit Indian-style. Being middle-aged, and not quite as limber as she was, he knew he would feel it tomorrow.

"Much better being eye-to-eye with you. . . . Now, when I was a kid, probably all of ten or eleven, my buddy Jeff and I went to this Builders Emporium. Actually, the one that was right around the corner from here, on Katella."

"Oh, I remember it," Mary interjected. "You know it's been gone for years. Maybe twenty or more."

"As I was saying, Jeff and I wanted, of all things, these two matching headbands. They were white with an American flag on them; we thought they were the coolest thing ever. So we each stuffed one in our pocket and walked out the front door.

Once outside, we ran like the devil into the open field right
next to the store. After about two hundred yards, I slowed
down to a jog and eventually stopped. I looked around for
Jeff. No Jeff. Way back in the distance, there he was, but not
alone. A large man dressed in a dark jacket was holding onto
his arm. I thought . . ."

Nick paused, reaching for his wineglass on the side table.
He took a sip, deliberately keeping her in suspense.

"Yeah, and?"

"Did I tell you that this wine is pretty good?"

"Yeah, yeah, wine's great. What happened?" Mary asked,
almost frantic.

Nick took another sip.

"Oh, you're really funny," she said. "Second time tonight
you've done that stall tactic thing. Seriously now, go on."

"All right," he chuckled. "I did the only thing I could. I
walked back to him, fully aware of what was about to happen."

A smile crossed Mary's face. "Wow."

Nick smirked.

THE TWO REMAINED seated on the floor for the next two hours,
talking, listening to the radio, and occasionally pouring a fresh
glass of wine. Nick had never told anyone that story before. It
revealed something remarkable about himself, and Mary *got*
it, got him. She instantly heard his message loud and clear.
How noble it was to draw a line in the sand and apologize to
no one for it. It confirmed that even at such a young age, Nick
was a man of honor, owning up to any wrongdoing.

By contrast, as Nick understood, Mary's family lived on
the blurred edges of morality. Blaming others was a common
trait, especially with her mother. Mary told him, on more than

one occasion, how her mother had come home announcing the incompetence of today's youth. How they didn't know math and never correctly counted out the change. That was a big mistake since any till shortage would come out of the employee's own pocket.

Her mother would go on and on about the cashier at the local Shell station. How she had given him a five-dollar bill for gas and received change for a twenty. And, yes, she kept the money and the gas, laughing all the way home. Honesty only had importance when others spoke to her mother.

Nick rose to stretch his legs. He suddenly felt the effects of the wine, not powerfully, but enough to loosen him up.

He asked, "Do you have any music we can listen to?"

"Tons of stuff. Who do you like?" Mary stood up, smoothing out the wrinkles of her dress with her hands.

"Something on the slow side, mellow."

She looked at him, as if deciphering his intent, "Oooh, I see." She lightly touched his arm. "The real Nicky finally reveals himself."

He inadvertently had stumbled on his words again. About to speak, Mary put her finger to her lips and whispered, "Shhhh, I have the perfect one."

She walked over to the large wooden wall unit and opened one of its cabinet doors. She pulled out a CD and shut the cabinet, deliberately keeping it hidden from him. She inserted the CD into the player and fiddled with the volume during the musical intro, first up, and then down a bit, until the singer crooned his first words.

"Flawless," she murmured to herself as she gently started to sway to the music's rhythm. She didn't turn around; she knew he was watching.

Nick didn't recognize the artist, but liked the beat and tone of the crooner's voice. The moment was right. He approached her from behind and slipped his arm around her waist. The silky fabric felt thin. Mary leaned back onto him, arching her neck to look into his eyes. She turned. Taking her left hand, Nick led her to the center of the room. He pulled her close, wanting her. They danced, feeling each other's pulse.

Mary rested her head on his chest, encircling him with her arms. No words were spoken as to the ease in which they cast into each other's body. The scent of coconuts rose from Mary's hair. Nick breathed in heavily, inhaling her essence, the moment.

Dancing—it's only an excuse to hold her.

Thirteen

Life according to Mary: No one to hear.

THE *LEGACY* BOOK: Pages 89–92

Mary found herself floating in front of her grandpa Heil. She was light as a feather, her feet hovering above the mobile home's cheap carpet. From the kitchen she heard her grandma's voice.

"Marty, I hear you snoring like a bull in a ring. You got about five minutes till supper. Heil, you hear me?"

The old man roused from his nap. "Yah, I hear ya, Cecil."

"Good. Get yourself washed up."

"Uh-huh." He closed his eyes.

Mary watched, familiar with the surroundings, yet it felt somehow different. A shadowy presence came over her. Then she remembered.

"No! Not him. Grampa, you have to wake up. Please, wake up!" Mary screamed in terror.

He couldn't hear her; no one could.

Grandpa Heil's face instantly turned black. Then his facial features—wrinkles, eyes, mouth, eyebrows, and the usual five o'clock stubble along the chin—all disappeared into darkness.

Grandmother Cecil walked into the room.

"For goodness' sake," she mumbled, seeing him in the recliner. Patting him on the shoulder, she said, "Marty, supper's on. Why didn't you—"

His head slumped to the left. His elbow slipped off the arm of the chair and dangled.

"Marty?" She stood back, frightened.

"Do something, Grandma!" Mary's words vanished without sound as she watched his life fade away.

Grandma Cecil bent over him, and with trembling hands, shook him fiercely. Getting no response, she crumpled to the ground, holding his hand.

His time had come. His wish fulfilled, he passed in his sleep.

Mary woke from the dream crying and cold. Her first instinct was to call Grandmama Matos and talk about the nightmare. She thought twice. Both grandmothers already knew. Mom would know soon enough, tomorrow. There was nothing she could do.

Fourteen

At some point the date had to come to an end. They had shared two kisses: the peck on the cheek at the beginning of the night, actually more of a calming gesture than a real kiss, and then later, the full-mouthed kiss that had provoked unexpected regret in Mary. Nick had taken it all in stride, displaying his usual nothing-fazes-me persona, although he had set his sights on a good night kiss.

Mary was polite, leading him to the front door. Nick stepped out onto the porch, expecting her to follow. He turned to find Mary leaning against the door frame, arms loosely crossed, watching him with a devilish grin. He read her body language and raised his eyebrows.

Taking it as a challenge, Nick turned on the charm—what little he had.

"Thank you for the wonderful dinner and especially the talk. I had a great time," he said with a smirk of his own.

Mary softened, unfolding her arms, and reached out to stroke Nick's arm. Without hesitation, Nick stepped forward and delicately placed his hands on Mary's shoulders, gazing into her eyes. Her attention was on his lips. Their bodies curved into each other. She melted against him, holding him tightly in a hug.

"You are welcome," she whispered. "It's so nice to have you here. It's been such a long time since there's been a man in my home. Thank you for coming."

Mary released herself from the embrace to take in his big brown eyes. Nick's right hand moved to her cheek, and then slowly caressed her jawline down to the nape of her neck. Tenderly, he tilted her head back, and they kissed. Their tongues tasted each other's breath. Hands moved slowly and passionately over each other. Moments later, their lips separated, damp traces lingered while half smiles took the place of their desire.

"I'll call you tomorrow," Nick said, taking a step backward, still holding her hand.

"You better. Now go home," she said, shooing him away with her words, although her eyes said otherwise.

Letting go of her hand, he cracked a big toothy grin.

"Good night, Mary," he turned and started the walk to his car. Then he abruptly stopped and turned back to her.

"I forgot to leave the ring with you."

"Please, dear, keep it for me. I know it's safe with you." Mary smiled.

Nick ran back to her and gave her a quick kiss. "Good night again," he said. Mary's left hand trailed in the air as he backed away.

At the car, he took a last glance back. Mary, once again, was leaning against the door frame, arms crossed. She gave him an abbreviated wave. Nick returned the wave and drove off.

ON THE SHORT drive home, Nick immersed himself in the night's experiences, but mostly the big kiss—replaying every detail: the feel of her soft lips as they pressed against his, how their bodies gently converged, hands everywhere, her essence surrounding him. Nick lifted a fistful of his shirt and took a big whiff; her feminine floral scent was on him.

He was content with the way the date ended. Nick had never been the type of guy who was into that whole "getting it" thing. Had that kiss gone on any longer, he might have done something he would regret tomorrow. Sure, being a man, he would have loved for things to have progressed further, but that wasn't who he was. The notion one should be in love before hopping into bed might be old-fashioned, but it was a principle he held onto. It was like smoking a good cigar— once you found it, you wait for just the right moment, then light it up and savor its every nuance.

The greatest moments of life can come suddenly.

Fifteen

Over the next several weeks Nick talked to Mary every night. Whether it was a five- or thirty-minute call, hearing her voice was enough for him. He had fallen into her trap—as habits do breed dependence. Regardless, Nick liked the routine.

They spent most weekends together: going to dinner, seeing the occasional movie, and sharing in intimate conversations accompanied by a few sips of wine. Time was on their side.

* * * * * *

Sunday's gift.

Returning from a quick trip to the market, Mary pulled her red '03 Chevy Cavalier onto the driveway and immediately noticed a shiny silver package on her front porch. After guiding the car into the garage, she turned off the engine. The motor sputtered and eventually died, as if out of breath.

"I'm really going to have to take this in—soon," she mumbled to herself.

It was not a cool car by any means. Even when it first appeared on the showroom floor, critics considered it "bland." Not exactly an overwhelming endorsement for one of America's premier auto manufacturers. And then, through the years, Mary couldn't be bothered to wax it and ignored the car's service maintenance recommendations. She believed that oil changes were an unnecessary evil and merely another way for big corporations to steal money from the masses. For her, there was never enough time to fight every cause. After all, it was only a car.

Mary opened the trunk and hauled out the three plastic grocery bags. Stepping through the back door, she plopped her purse on the glass table on her way into the kitchen. After dropping the grocery bags off, she excitedly ran to the front door.

Smiling, she opened the door. She looked down at the rectangular box wrapped in a heavy, high-quality silver paper. Tied with white ribbon, a single bow was perfectly centered on top. Tucked under the bow was a small envelope with her name on it. She took the box inside, leaving the door open.

Taking a seat in the living room, she placed the box on the table in front of her. Feeling suddenly nervous, her hands began to shake while she reached for the envelope. When Mary was a child, she received gifts only twice a year, her birthday and Christmas. There were never any surprise shopping outings or "just because" presents. Even in her marriage, other than flowers on Valentine's Day, gifts were an unusual event. To receive something for no reason at all didn't make sense.

She pulled the plain white card from the envelope. She felt her heart race as she unfolded it. The neat penmanship spelled out:

Open me up to see the most beautiful treasure in the world.

It wasn't signed. But Mary knew it was from him. She took her time unwrapping it, anxious, yet secretly enjoying the experience.

She carefully peeled away the paper, trying her best not to tear it. It was certainly too pretty to throw away. Delicately, she folded the wrapping and placed it out of her way under the coffee table. Picking up the box, she placed it on her lap and used her fingernail to cut through the tape along the top. Mary took a look inside, her hazel eyes sparkling back at herself, slightly tearing up at the thought of Nick's attention to every detail. Inside the box was a small hand mirror.

As she lifted it out, she read the words on the glass written with a dark red marker:

It's your heart
I want most.

She clutched the mirror to her chest. A single tear rolled down. She gave a nervous little-girl giggle. Mary too was taken.

She looked down into the box again—there was more.

Within, under the parchment paper, were three red roses, each in its own glass vial. Placed next to the roses, a small box of Ghirardelli chocolates, her favorite.

"Oh, Nicky, you sure know how to woo a girl," she said out loud, her voice trembling.

Mary leaned back, holding the flowers in one hand and the mirror in the other. She drew the roses up to her nose and breathed in deeply. Exhaling, she couldn't help but be in awe of this man, who was doting on her. She dared to wish for his countenance and was sure that if she could see his soul, it would be pure white with large feathered wings. Everything she had dreamed for herself seemed to be coming true.

She breathed in again and smiled. Then she remembered . . . and her smile disappeared.

You can't escape from who you are.

Sixteen

Life according to Mary: No getting over the rainbow.

THE *LEGACY* BOOK: Pages 104–107

Although infrequent, the dreams were an intense part of Mary's adolescence. As she grew older, the dreams increased in regularity and severity. She would discuss each one in great detail with Grandmama Matos. Mary longed for a magical word or phrase that would dispel the tormenting guilt from within. Grandmama Matos tried to comfort her, and superficially, she succeeded. But privately, Mary was suffering. When she dreamed of someone being hurt or witnessed a death, and unable to alter a fate, it plagued her. The dark images persisted long after each dream. As it had been for the women before her, coping became a way of life.

Mary last visited Grandmama on a Sunday afternoon, the day before her ninety-eighth birthday. Always happy to see Mary, she greeted her with a warm hold. In spite of her advanced age, Grandmama Matos had all of her mental faculties, although walking was another story. She had her left knee drained several times a month to alleviate a persistent fluid buildup. The constant pain made it difficult for her to get around.

"Ah, *meu* baby, you looks so beautiful," Grandmother Matos said, as they took a seat.

"Thank you, Grandmama. And you look great too," Mary lied, but always out of love.

They sat in the kitchen, uncomfortably empty of the opulent furnishings Grandmama had once owned. The kitchen chairs were old and covered with thick, protective plastic. The design of the fabric was impossible to make out under the opaque, discolored plastic. The kitchen table had been at one time white linoleum, but was now yellowed, with a heavily used ashtray for a centerpiece.

"I had another one last night," Mary said.

"I know. First, I give a gift."

Grandmama Matos eased herself out of her chair and hobbled out of the room. She returned clutching *the book* to her chest.

"No, Grandmama," Mary said.

"It's a time. You're all grown up, have a man—"

"Please." Mary begged, not ready to accept what it meant.

"You take now," she said, placing the book on the table.

"I'm not going to take it home."

"I saw it too, last night dream. It's done."

She reached over and patted Mary's hands. Tears rolled down Mary's face. She was coming to grips with the fact that this would be the last time she would see her Grandmama.

. . . and it came to be. As she had dreamt, Grandmama Matos died of heart failure that same night. The Legacy book was now Mary's.

Part 2

Seventeen

Of things left behind . . .

NICK HUGGED STEPHANIE. She felt skinny, too thin to hold her already delicate frame. The stench of booze oozed from her pores, screaming of another one of her all-night binges. As he released her, her head swiveled backward like a bobblehead doll's before settling back into its rightful position.

"Thank you for calling me for lunch. I've been thinking a lot about you lately," she said.

Unfazed by her comment, Nick pulled out her chair and took a seat himself. He had long since learned not to trust her words when she had been drinking and especially the morning afterward. Stephanie sat, crossing her legs, and leaned inward.

In the short time since he'd last seen her, Stephanie's appearance had changed dramatically. Her face, once youthful and healthy, was now gaunt, her skin tone a morgue gray. Her hair, which, during their marriage, had been flawlessly arranged, was now straggly, with a streak of coarse gray down her middle part. Black half-moons underscored her bloodshot eyes. He didn't remember her having so many wrinkles. She knew he knew.

Nick cracked a half smile. "You know I call you every time I'm coming back home."

"Then Las Vegas is still your home, huh?" Stephanie smirked.

"Yeah, in a way." Nick stopped short, not wanting to explain himself. He had never discussed with Stephanie why he left Las Vegas. And having experience with her debating skills, he didn't want to waste his energy on the topic.

"Damn, Nick, you look good. What'd you do, lose some weight?"

"No, haven't dropped a pound. But aren't you kind to say so." He paused. "So, how are you really doing, Steph?"

"Why? Do you think there's something wrong with me? You do, don't you? I shouldn't have—"

"No, wondering, that's all. Remember, we *were* married for a long time, and I *do* care. And that's never going to change."

"Oh . . . Thank you." Stephanie looked away. "Hey, how about we get a drink?"

Nick ordered an iced tea, Stephanie a beer.

After their fill of crawdads and king crab legs, the conversation turned sober.

"Okay, Steph, I have to ask. Are you still with the coward?" Nick didn't mince his words.

"I wish you would stop calling him that. And you know I am."

"Well, I was hoping for a different answer. . . . Seriously though, what are you doing? I can't believe you went back to him." Nick's expression showed his obvious disapproval.

"Miss." Stephanie raised her arm at the waitress. "Another beer over here."

Nick turned around to the waitress who was approaching. "No more beer. I believe we're done. Thank you anyway." He shot Stephanie a stern glare.

"Look, Stephanie, no amount of alcohol is going to make it right with him. Are you forgetting about last year? How you ran through the streets screaming for help and ended up on my doorstep?"

"Well, yeah."

"How your mascara streamed down your cheeks? You were shaking and shivering from the trouncing he had just put on you. We weren't sure if you were going to live. You *do* remember that, don't you?"

"Yeah, we had a few bad times. But, it's different now. He's not like that anymore. He's changed."

Nick clenched his jaw. He remembered that night, how Russell had beaten her senseless, and then chased her out of their apartment, completely naked. She ran more than a mile to his home, bruised and still bleeding. And if it hadn't been for his sister Shannon and her husband Jesse visiting, he would have gone over and killed the coward himself. Jesse had stopped him with a hard slap to the back of the head, after which, a bit of a tussle ensued. Pinning Jesse against the wall, Nick came out of his stupor.

"People like that don't change."

"You keep saying that. But you're wrong, Nick."

"Statistics bear me out."

"I don't want to talk to you about this anymore."

"Steph, don't wait until the next time. It *can* get uglier, I've seen it. You need to leave him."

"I need another beer, miss." Stephanie waved her hand, avoiding his eyes.

"How about this—I can get you some counseling. I'll pay for it." Nick leaned in. "I've got friends who could get you the best help in town."

Redirecting her attention to Nick, Stephanie said, "Help? I don't need any help. The only thing I need right now is a beer and change of subject."

"A beer? Seriously, *that's* your biggest problem—a beer?" Nick ran his hand through his hair.

"Yep."

She ordered another beer. Nick held his tongue; he had had his say.

I've quit doing time for you—starting now.

Eighteen

Nick rolled over onto his side, pulling the covers up over his head in an effort to muffle the sound. The continuous ring of his home phone echoed in his head like the effects of a bad hangover, pounding and throbbing. Arriving home late from a quick trip to Las Vegas, and then staying up until two in the morning had done him in. And sure, that third *rammer* certainly hadn't helped matters.

A rammer typically was the last drink of the night, and usually the strongest. Straight-up alcohol—whiskey, bourbon, or scotch were the accepted beverages. In Nick's case, he embellished the rule. Nothing was better than a well-mixed Manhattan, in a bucket, on the rocks, skipping the dash of Angostura bitters, with a single maraschino cherry. He had three last drinks. It helped his writing, especially after seeing Stephanie as she was. He understood his own hypocrisy.

The phone stopped ringing—*finally, silence.* He threw off the covers, lay on his back, bare-chested, in boxers, and began to pry open his bloodshot eyes. Then the ringing started again.

"Who in the hell is calling me at this time of the morning?!" Nick glanced at the clock. "It's 6:12, on a Sunday. You gotta be frickin' kidding me."

Nick stretched for the phone. He answered in a gruff voice. "Yeah, what is it?"

"Nick?"

Still in a fog, his pitch deepened. "Yeah, of course it's me!" *Okay, lady, you called me; who else would it be?* he thought.

"Nick, I'm so glad you're home. I tried your cell phone; it must be off or something." Her speech quickened. "I need to see you."

When he realized it was Mary, his tone instantly softened, "Oh, sweetie, I'm not really awake right now. Later would be a whole lot better. Besides, aren't we having dinner tonight?"

"No, no, Nick. I have to see you right now."

"Why? What's wrong?" He sat up, eyes immediately wide open.

"I can't say over the phone. But, please, you have to come over right now. . . . Please."

"Are you okay? Is this an emergency?"

Mary hesitated. "Oh, um . . . please, I need to see you before I forget. Okay?"

Sensing her desperation, he replied, "Sure thing, give me a couple of minutes."

"Nicky, thank you so much."

"Mary, it'll be all right," Nick said confidently. "I promise, no matter what it is."

They both hung up.

IT TOOK HIM seven minutes to shower, change, and make a cup of instant coffee. Out the door, cup in hand, heart pounding, Nick wondered what kind of problem he would be facing. Yes, he was a fixer.

He knocked on her front door, hair still wet. His untucked, collared shirt hung down like a sheet on an unmade bed—rumpled and rippled. Nick stood, self-assured, peering through the window in the door. Mary opened it and at once jumped into his arms, her eyes red. She didn't release him, holding him tightly as if her life depended on it.

"Thank you, God, thank you," she whispered into his chest. "Oh, Nick, I'd die if anything ever happened to you. I love you so much."

Tears flowed from Mary as she pressed her head forcefully against his chest, her arms clutching him. Nick returned the embrace, dumbfounded, especially by her last statement. That was the first time either of them had used the word "love."

"I'm fine." Nick brushed off the comment and tried pulling back, wanting to see her face.

Mary didn't let go; instead, only tightened her grip. Tears continued to fall, followed by deep sobs. Her hold ever unyielding, Nick surrendered to it, not seeking any answers. A calm silence fell between them. For the next few minutes, they stood, joined in an unspoken understanding. The morning sun warmed Nick's back, sparrows chirped in the background, and the smell of blooming jasmine permeated the air from the morning dew. It was at that exact moment Nick recognized his life had been inarguably altered. He was in love with this strange, unpredictable woman.

Reading what was written on his heart.

Nineteen

Thoughts of Stephanie crept in more often than he liked. And now with Mary, realizing he could be happy sowed new seeds of fear. Nick questioned why this gorgeous, vivacious woman, who could have anyone she desired, had chosen him to love. He wasn't the most attractive guy anymore, and she had no idea of his financial position, at least to his knowledge. So, then, why him?

Nick had been doing fine before her, resigning himself to a life of seclusion, and all that went with it. The solitary meals, the quiet nights, waking up alone were all things he had come to expect. Then, out of nowhere, she appeared and changed everything. Of course, Mary had a few quirks of her own. But who doesn't?

It's amazing how the mind can shape-shift a strongly held belief to alleviate the ache of loneliness. How easily the past can be readily forgotten when someone new tugs on the heart—that's the wonder of love.

* * * * * *

WITHOUT A WORD, Mary released her grip on Nick, stepped back, and then pulled him inside the house. She had him take a seat in the living room. Nick remained as always—quiet, watchful, patient.

She paced in front of him, only stopping to wipe away the last of the fears from her cheeks. Without looking at him, she began to talk.

"All right, I know this is going to sound a little bizarre . . ." she turned to meet his eyes, "but you have to trust me on what I'm going to say."

Nick continued to observe, studying her expressions, then leaned forward, resting his elbows on his knees.

"Early this morning I had a dream." She paused, hands trembling. "And it was about you."

Nick's forehead wrinkled with bewilderment.

"You see, when I have this type of dream, it's not like a regular person's dream." Mary's hands shook. "And it always ends up with something bad happening."

"Hold on," Nick interjected. "All of this is about some dream that you had about me?"

"Yes, but give me a minute, so that you can understand. You have no idea how hard this is."

Nick sat back, crossing his arms.

"Thanks. Now, in my dream, we were at your house. We had finished eating, and we were sitting in the living room talking. I don't remember exactly about what. Anyway, we were talking, and then the doorbell rang. You got up to answer it. I'm watching you the entire time. You opened the door and looked outside, and then back at me. At that precise moment, your face turned all black."

Nick waited.

"And . . .?" he asked.

"And, that's it."

Oh shit, I'm in love with a nut job, he thought.

Mary sat down on the coffee table directly in front of him. She placed her hands on his knees.

"Please, hear me, Nicky," she squeezed nervously. "These dreams are real. They give me insight into another level of consciousness. My grandmama Matos believed they were a window into the future. And any way you want to look at it, the dreams have tangible life consequences to them. Something bad is going to happen to you. Yeah, I know this sounds crazy, but I'm not. Really."

Nick leaned forward, caressed her hair in a comforting manner. Mary's head drooped, and she drew her hands off his knees to stop them from shaking.

"Oh, sweetie, nothing's going to happen to me. Everything is good, great even. To be honest, this is the happiest I've been since I can remember. I like my job, like where I live, and I've got the greatest girl in the world. I'm the one who's lucky here."

He lifted Mary's chin, leaning in lightly to kiss her lips. She nudged closer and slipped to his side, so they were cheek to cheek.

She whispered softly, "Oh, Nick, you have no idea."

Mary broke away and stood up. She walked to the opposite side of the room where a large walnut bookshelf filled the space. She carefully touched and tapped several of the book spines, then murmured something indistinguishable, keeping her back to him. The bookshelf held hundreds of books, making the room warm and inviting. She pulled out a book and sat next to Nick, almost in his lap. She placed the coffee table-sized book on the table in front of them.

The book's cover appeared to be made of cowhide or other animal skin. Three dark rings marred the leather, probably left by wineglasses. The title was engraved in gold leaf: *Legacy*.

"Nick, like I asked you before, I need you to trust me on this. Please listen to my words before you turn into Mr. Detective. Okay?"

Nick nodded, saying nothing, arms crossed again, eyes squarely on the book.

"Good."

Mary opened it a few pages in. Starting on a left-hand page was the beginning of a family tree, containing a multitude of limbs and branches. Each one had its own handwritten entries of names, dates, and locations. The tree's limbs extended to the next page and several pages beyond that.

"This book details my family's genealogy, Dad's side only. My mom's side, for better or worse, is the normal one," Mary sighed. "Anyway, look here at all of these women. Every one of them had what I have, a sort of prophecy gift, but in the worst way. Our lineage goes back centuries.

"Right here," Mary pointed to a branch in the middle of the first page of the family tree that read AD 1438. "It's because of her."

Nick frowned.

"Let me clarify, okay?" she paused. "Back in those days, my early ancestors were poor and traveled from one village to the next, mostly between Portugal, Spain, and a little in North Africa. They earned money as entertainers, musicians, and selling trinkets they'd make, like charms and other jewelry. You might consider them gypsies. Most people came to them because of their mystical practices—for healings, magical potions, that type of thing. They were pagans."

Turning several well-worn pages, Mary stopped at a clearly marked historical section titled "The Affliction Chronicles." She took a peek at Nick. Seeing no reaction, she returned to the book.

"Now this is what I wanted to show you." She stopped, momentarily focusing on the page. "Okay, yeah, this was written hundreds of years ago and has been handed down from one woman to the next, and then to me." She began to read a portion of the account.

In AD 1452, Pope Nicolas V, being a self-righteous man, issued a Papal Bull of declarement for the enslavement of all Saracens, pagans, other unbelievers and enemies of Christ wherever they doth be. The ruler, Afonso V of Portugal, in accordance with the decree, commenced harvesting up of the multitudes, thereby consigning many unto perpetual slavery.

The great and noble Ametist Eduardo Roman . . .

Mary looked up. "This is where it started, in our bloodline." Nick remained stoic.

The great and noble Ametist Eduardo Romano, leader of the assembly of Vento and great ancestral father, doth bartered his lone child, Mia, thus sparing the traveling faction from prosecution and thereof enslavement. General Fernando Almeirim, representing Afonso V of Portugal, doth exchange for the girl, granted the assembly of Vento clemency. Honoring her father, Mia, without complaint, left with the General. The assembly of Vento sojourned to the next village bearing the paper of purity.

Hence, in order to conform and conceal the assembly's underlying truths, the families of Vento disguised their religious patronage. Many became known by Christian names whilst others converted to Christianity.

One night, after year two, as General Fernando Almeirim slept, Mia garnered a knife and cut her master's throat. His blood drained whilst she made her escape.

The General's bereaved mother, Ester, and eldest brother, Henry, sought Mia to exact revenge. Once found, the same knife Mia had used to murder Fernando, brother Henry used to slice her neck. The wound Henry inflicted was not deepened, leaveth Mia alive. Ester harvested droplets of Mia's blood into a word-inscribed wooden bowl. Dropping the bowl at the feet of Mia, Ester spat a curse on the Romano family.

The imprecation: That each first-born female henceforth shall foresee evils by the blackness of their own dreams.

"The two-faced part of the story is that the general's family themselves were pagans." Mary glanced at Nick. "So, there it is."

Nick stared at the page trying to analyze the type of calligraphy—wondering if the rounded shapes and swirls fit the time period.

"And that's why you're here—the reason for my urgency. Whenever I dream of someone with a black face, it means something bad *will* happen to that person, and last night, I dreamed of you. They're called black dreams."

"Interesting," Nick finally said, forcing a smile. "Mary, look at me. I'm fine."

"Yeah, I know, right now. But the family's curse always comes true."

Nick scowled.

"Well, let's say you're right, and there's some sort of dark voodoo evil coming my way. Don't worry, I can handle it."

Nick lightly touched her hand.

Mary pulled away, putting distance between them.

"Maybe you should go," she stated firmly.

"Now, Mary, this isn't like you."

"No, Nick, I want you to go."

"Seriously?"

"Dead serious."

Nick got up and was out the door. He could feel her eyes on him. He didn't turn back.

What you feed on is what you're full of.

Twenty

What was that? he thought.

IT WASN'T AS if Nick hadn't come across odd behavior before. As an officer, one of the weirdest cases involved a woman whom he had arrested for prostitution. Admittedly, Las Vegas and prostitution are not exactly strange bedfellows. But it was the reasoning behind it—what the woman called her "righteous good deeds"—that made it unforgettable.

She was in her early thirties, married, a churchgoing mother of three, and a well-respected member of the community. The woman claimed she was fulfilling *His* charge as commanded. Apparently, God wanted her to offer up her body for the benefit of the less fortunate—a seemingly altruistic sacrifice. Then, the proceeds were to be handed over to the church coffers anonymously.

She described in detail how God had spoken through the whisperings of the leaves in her backyard. God called to her only during times of orange-skied sunsets. The tree, a coolibah Eucalyptus, was the vehicle for His messages. During those chosen times, the tree's foliage would rustle in the evening breeze. She would carefully watch and listen as the leaves knocked and bounced off each other, producing a low murmur and the occasional high-pitched whistle. Each tone she interpreted as a clear spiritual instruction. According to the woman, whenever she failed one of His tests, the morning after, the lawn surrounding the tree would die from the roots up. The grass, previously a healthy lush green, turned brown, looking as if it had been scorched by fire. Her faith in God and His will vindicated her every action. Nick later confirmed that all monies she earned, had, in fact, been donated to her church.

Thus, by comparison, Mary's belief in black dreams wasn't all that bizarre. Okay, perhaps a bit. Still, to Nick, it was no more eccentric than certain religious sects speaking in tongues or conducting faith healings. To outsiders, such supernatural things gave rise to worldly rational skepticism. However, Nick, having personally experienced a spirit-filled church in action, thought differently. Perhaps Mary did possess the ability for prognostication, or, as she put it, a power born of a family curse.

* * * * * *

ONCE HOME, EXHAUSTED, he went back to bed. He shut his eyes. For two hours he tossed and turned from one side of the bed to the other, his mind in a constant churning state. Finally, having had enough, he got up.

Despite their argument, he assumed their date for that night was, nonetheless, *on.* He felt he had to do a little something extra to try to smooth things over. Yes, Nick the fixer wanted her, even as offbeat as she was. His first thought was to do the usual guy thing, buy some flowers or a small knickknack, but he had just done that. He had a bigger problem . . . how to apologize. Not for what he had said, but for how he had handled the entire conversation.

Nick sat down at the kitchen table and thought. Eventually, he grabbed a pen and paper and began. He had to reveal his heart. Their argument wasn't the real issue; it was him, again. He needed more out of himself.

He wrote:

> *Mary, my sweet, sweet Mary,*
> *mysterious as the moon shining down.*
> *I am the sea, tied and pulled by your gravity.*
> *I drown in your flashing eyes*
> *that see oceans deep into me and beyond.*
>
> *Mary, my sweet, sweet Mary,*
> *I want to breathe in your coconut scent*
> *and drink your lips of ripe cherries.*
> *You are a siren, entangling me in your long hair,*
> *bringing me to life, even as I lose my breath in your beauty.*
>
> *Mary, my sweet, sweet Mary,*
> *You hear what I don't say*
> *but listen for the words drumming in my chest.*

You are spring water to wash away my parched days.
Mary, sweet, lovely Mary, if truly mine, you will love all of me.

Feelings were easier on paper. Nick folded the sheet in three and placed it in an envelope.

Then he lay down on the couch for a short nap.

Love becomes love when it's given.

Twenty-one

Nick cut the stems of the summer bouquet, excluding any yellow ones, added the packet of flower preserver to the vase, and filled it with water. Once placed on the table, the arrangement with its orange sunflowers, red and white carnations, and violet daisies lent the room a festive air. He further adorned the table with his finest china dishes, cloth napkins, and polished silverware, all new and seldom used, finding their proper place. The envelope leaned conspicuously against the wineglass where Mary was to sit.

Nick's hands were wet with anticipation. Hours earlier the confirmation call had not gone as he had hoped—her responses were short and curt. Regardless, the night was about to happen. He felt unusually edgy, however. It had more to do with his heart and what he had to say.

There was a light tap on the door.

Nick jumped out of his comfy leather chair and turned down the CD player. It wasn't loud; however, he couldn't risk any distractions marring those first moments that could establish the tenor for the evening. He quickly fine-tuned the volume for background music, confident it would help soften the tension. Nick had chosen *Days of Future Passed* by the Moody Blues, a smooth and melodious album with poignant lyrics. Mary's timing was perfect, as one of Nick's favorite songs, "Evening: The Sunset/Twilight Time," began to play.

As he opened the door, Nick wasn't sure what to expect. Mary stood before him, expressionless, not even a blink. She clutched the *Legacy* book to her bosom; her feet were crossed at the ankles. The music, as low as it was, saturated the anxiety-filled silence between them.

Mary was dressed in a white and light orange dappled sundress with spaghetti straps that accentuated her flawless tanned skin. She was, once again, the sexiest thing Nick had ever seen. In a flash, he forgot about the weight of their prior conversation of who was right or wrong. He didn't care. All he knew was he'd be the one cursed if he didn't act.

"Wow, you look amazing and . . ." Nick couldn't control his mouth, something of a first for him. "Listen, before you come in, I want to apologize. I should have been a better man and—"

Mary gently placed the book on the ground and leaped into his arms, hugging him fiercely.

"No, I'm so sorry, Nicky. I should have used understanding words. I just love you so much that I never, *ever* want anything to happen to you. I'm absolutely in love with you," Mary exhaled sharply into Nick's chest.

"Oh no, it's me and—"

"Shhhh, don't say anything." Reaching up, Mary kissed him on the cheek.

"But, sweetie, I have to tell you that—"

"Hush now." Mary placed her index finger on his lips, and then slowly caressed his cheek. "Nicky, already I know."

Do you? Do you really know? Those three words I've said so rarely and have struggled to say to you. And yet, you've given me a pass on saying them. Oh, that's not going to happen.

Nick pulled her away, looking directly into her eyes. She looked down, deliberately avoiding his watchful intent.

"Mary, look at me."

Mary glanced up into his eyes with a terrified look on her face.

"Do you know that each night when I lay my head down, you are always my last thought? Then when I wake in the morning you are my first thought . . . actually, you take up more of my thoughts than you should."

Mary's eyes began to tear up and again searched for an opening to turn away.

"Please, don't," he said. "I'm not good at this and need your focus on me."

Mary turned her eyes back to him.

"You make me feel like I'm a high school kid," Nick said. "Like my first big crush. Happy. I hope to God—"

Abruptly, Nick stopped, suddenly self-conscious. He stroked her hair, releasing the aroma of the coconut conditioner. After two long breaths, he had to say it.

"Mary, I love you."

Tears rolled down Mary's cheeks as if she couldn't believe what she was hearing. She understood Nick was a man of few words, especially when it came to sentiment. Even from their first conversation, she determined hearing those words probably weren't in the cards. Accepting this, she had taken it upon herself to say it for both of them. In her heart, she had always known how he felt. Yet, to hear him say "I love you" was more than she could take. Tears streamed from her eyes, falling, finding their way onto her dress's cotton fabric. She couldn't speak; her lips were sealed in disbelief and overwhelming joy. Still, a smile emerged, exposing her soul, naked and pure.

"Nicky . . . I love you too," Mary whispered.

The music continued to play in the background. They swayed, holding each other in the doorway. All was right at the Pajak house.

The man inside took charge.

Twenty=two

Nick touched his face and felt lipstick smeared across his mouth as if put there by a child who had scrawled outside the lines with a red crayon. Once inside the house, Mary's perfume lingered everywhere, even overpowering the freshly cut bouquet of flowers. The *Legacy* book had been set on the coffee table in the TV room. She wanted him to read it, in his own time, to understand her truth.

WHEN THEY SAT down for dinner, Nick watched Mary's eyes as she saw the envelope. A quick smile crossed her face. She gently moved it away from her wineglass, saying nothing. Nick made no mention of it either. A playful game of chess ensued.

He gazed across the table, smiling, with good cause. He had been transformed from what he once was into someone he didn't know, but liked better. He held no reservations about his feelings for Mary and was thankful for every minute with her. His only wish, a self-serving deep secret, was simply to be loved again, and it seemed to have come true.

Nick was attentive to Mary's every word. He listened as she described how she had developed a concentration problem at work. How her brother and boss, Kent, had to repeat himself two or three times before his directive finally stuck.

Mary said, "After all, Nicky, it's your fault. I would sit there hour after hour, staring off in the distance, dreaming of you."

Nick sat, grinning.

Mary's eyes were steady on his lips. "Could you love me for life?"

Nick's eyebrows arched. "Uh, I want to believe I can."

"Now, that's not very reassuring." Mary paused, realizing the underpinning of her question. "Wait, you didn't think I was asking you to marry me?" Her cheeks immediately flushed a rosy red. "Oh, forget it. I don't know what I was thinking."

"Hmmmm." Nick chuckled at the sight of her discomfiture. Yet, on a subconscious level, she might have been testing him. He did love her but wasn't ready for the next step. In spite of what they had shared, she was still an enigma to him, a riddle for which he had no answers. He felt like he was missing pieces of the puzzle—though he couldn't quite pinpoint what they were.

During their time together, she had only spoken once of her former husband, Stan Berean. According to Mary, he was gifted with a brilliant mind and never forgot a fact.

At Ohio State, Stan had been class valedictorian and later had gone on to become the youngest managing partner of Arthur Anderson, one of the big eight accounting firms at the time. They had met at a pool party in Palm Springs during spring break, his senior year. Mary, two years younger, occasionally attended classes at Orange Coast College, the local junior college. Her main interest at school had been getting the scoop on the "when and where" of the next party. Intellectually, she had been no match for Stan. However, he could only dream of a girl like Mary.

They were married four months after they met. Mary dutifully followed his every step, being the good wife. Eventually, Stan's ballooning ego, and other women, became more than she could handle. Their love was lost somewhere along his path to success. After eleven protracted years, the marriage ended ugly.

Mary disclosed very little about her mother or any other family member. Other than the compliment about her brother and Grandmama Matos, she never brought up the past. Nick's intuition told him not to question her too closely. He hated having to "get all detective" on her, as she would say. He figured she'd talk about it when she was ready.

Nor did Nick share much about his past life with Stephanie or other intimate family details, though he did fill her in whenever he saw Stephanie, but usually after the fact. Mary seemed to receive the information with an ever-increasing protectiveness of their relationship. As soon as Nick brought up any business trip to Las Vegas, the first words out of Mary's mouth were about Stephanie. "Did you see her? How'd she look?" Nick spoke the truth, keeping his responses unemotional and concise, not wanting an inquisition.

AFTER DINNER, NICK pulled out her chair and motioned for her to follow him.

Mary hesitated, looking longingly at the envelope on the table. She rose, glanced at him, and back at the envelope.

A low chuckle escaped Nick.

"You're just so pleased with yourself, aren't you?" she said. "And wipe that smug look off your face."

"What?" His chuckle turned into a hearty laugh.

"Are you going to give it to me or not?"

"What?"

"The envelope, you tease," she said.

Nick sidestepped back to the table, stretched around Mary, and picked up the envelope.

"Oh, you mean this?"

Mary paused, bowed her head slightly, eyes wide open, giving him a puppy dog look.

"All right, Nicky, if you're not ready to give it to me, that's okay. I understand, that is . . . if it *is* for me." She brought her hands up, covering her heart.

Oh, you're good. You could've opened it anytime you liked, Nick thought. *But now, you haven't seen anything yet.*

"Thanks, you're right. I'll put it away for another time," he said.

Nick turned to walk away. Mary reached out and grabbed his arm.

"Okay, you win. Give it to me. You know how I love your gifts."

Nick held the envelope above his head, goading her.

"Then come and get it."

Mary had no chance of reaching the envelope, but she did have a weapon that Nick couldn't resist. Craftily, she drew close, placed her arms around him, and hugged. Then, rising onto her tiptoes, she kissed his neck. She made no motion for his outstretched arm.

Nick melted, succumbing to her seductive powers. She knew how to use her feminine wiles, and he was severely outgunned. Mary's light caresses overwhelmed him. He lowered his arm.

"Here," he said, surrendering the envelope. "Let's take this into the other room. You can open it there."

She pushed it back to him.

"Oh no, my darling Nicky, I don't need to open it. You've already told me by your actions. . . . But, if I *do* open it, *you* have to read it to me. I want to hear every word out of your own mouth."

In a quick reversal, Mary led Nick by the hand into the living room, where she took a seat on the couch. She flipped her hair back flirtatiously, and then leaned forward, eyes centered on him.

"Okay, I'm ready. Read on, my love."

Nick stood stiffly before her, uneasy, wondering what had just happened. He pulled the single sheet of paper out of the unsealed envelope. He felt the wetness in the palms of his hands as he brought the paper to meet his eyes. His left hand flopped listlessly, as if he had just received a bad final exam score.

"Ah, now, be kind." Nick paused in disbelief at what he was about to do. "To tell you the truth, you're the first person I've ever shown anything I've ever written."

"Oooh, Nicky, since you wrote it, I'm sure I will love it. Please, go ahead." She grinned.

Nick raised the paper again and began:

> *Mary, my sweet, sweet Mary,*
> *mysterious as the moon shining down.*
> *I am the sea, tied and pulled by your gravity.*
> *I drown in your flashing eyes*
> *that see oceans deep into me and beyond.*

He stopped, exhaled heavily, switched his weight to the opposite side, and continued.

> *Mary, my sweet, sweet Mary,*
> *I want to breathe in your coconut scent*
> *and drink your lips of—*

The doorbell rang. Nick instantly stopped.

"Who could that be? I'm not expecting anyone," he said, grateful for the interruption. He picked up the envelope and stuffed the poem back inside, folded it in half, and then put it in his back pants pocket as he walked to the front door. Mary sat, shoulders slumped in abject disappointment.

Peering through the peephole, Nick saw a police officer.

Uninvited.

Twenty=three

No one likes police showing up at their front door . . . especially uninvited. And to make matters worse, a late-night visit in the middle of a romantic dinner à deux. As a police officer, Nick had made many of these late-night "informed status" calls. Showing no emotion, he would impart what was usually ominous information. His first beat partner told him, "If your phone or doorbell rings after ten p.m., it's never good news."

NICK'S HEART RACED. He opened the door.

"May I help you, Officer?" Nick asked.

"Mr. Nicholas James Pajak?" said the uniformed man. Nick was momentarily blinded by the light reflecting off the officer's polished brass badge.

"Yes?"

From behind the officer, a second man emerged and stepped onto the porch. Nick instantly recognized the distinctive swagger of a plainclothes detective.

"Good evening, sir," he said, taking charge. "I apologize for the interruption to your evening, especially due to the lateness of the hour. I'm Detective Dave Sherman from the Las Vegas Metropolitan Police Department, and this here is Officer Darling from the City of Orange."

Nick unconsciously stepped outside, extending his hand, first to the officer, and then to the detective.

"It's always nice to meet a fellow detective from my old stomping grounds. Old Towne precinct, by any chance?" Nick's stress levels rose as they shook hands.

"No sir. Out of the new headquarters on the other side of the I-15."

Releasing the detective's firm grip, Nick leaned back, propping himself against the door frame. In an effort to calm himself, he began to profile Officer Darling who had stepped back off the porch. Officer Darling was a rotund man, of medium height, five-ten, older, early fifties, with graying temples. He carried himself with great confidence, presumably the result of a lifetime's experience on the force. His retreat signaled the gravity of the visit and his subordinate role.

"Do you have a few minutes?" Detective Sherman asked. "We're here on official business."

"I see. Come in." Nick's neck muscles stiffened as the detective walked past him into the house.

"Mr. Pajak, are you alone?" Officer Darling asked from beyond.

"No, my girlfriend's in the other room."

"Does she live here with you?"

"No."

"Can you please ask her to come to the door?" Officer Darling remained off the porch, right hand on his gun, though it looked to be more out of habit than out of any expectation of using it.

Focused on Officer Darling's hand, Nick yelled out of the side of his mouth, "Mary, I need you to come out here."

Mary rounded the corner.

"What now?" her voice rose, agitated. "I'm not going to let you get away with—" she stopped midsentence upon seeing the man standing in the hall and the shadowy outline of another outside.

"Ma'am, I need you to step outside with me," said Officer Darling, moving onto the porch. "And can you please bring any of your personal belongings with you, ma'am."

"Nick, what's going on here?" She glanced at Nick.

"It'll be fine, Mary, go ahead," he said, trying to reassure her.

Mary picked up her purse from the foyer table and sauntered past Nick, giving him *the look*. All three men noticed.

Oh shit. Detective, arrest me now. I'm better off in jail, Nick thought.

Mary exited with a second glare back at Nick. Nick ignored her and led the detective into the living room.

"Sorry about that," the detective said. Nick pointed to the couch.

"Um-hmm," Nick muttered sarcastically, and sat in his leather chair, to the right of the couch.

Detective Sherman had a clean-cut professional look tailored for an intimidating presence. He wore gray slacks, a blue shirt, a skinny solid-black tie, and a matching black blazer. The pants and blazer appeared to be worn deliberately snug so as to show off his muscular physique, an unmistakable warning not to provoke this man. He stood about six-two, seemed to have no neck, and was as bald as a newborn. A fifteen-inch scar, starting at his right temple, went around his ear and down to the nape of his neck. His shield, which hung on his black leather belt, flashed when his jacket opened. His eyes were a light blue, which only served to underscore his menacing outer shell.

Detective Sherman reached into his blazer and pulled out a small notepad and pen. He wasted no time.

"Mr. Pajak, do you have any weapons in the house?"

"Of course."

"How many and where are they?" The detective jotted something down with a custom silver metal pen.

"Detective, your scar, what happened?"

The detective stopped writing, looked over at Nick, seemingly taken off his game, and then just as quickly returned to his notebook.

"Please, sir, how many guns and where are they?"

"Huh? Okay. I got a Sig Sauer P-2-20 and Colt M4 short barrel. Also, a .22. All of them are locked away in the gun safe. Why?"

"And what about the Ruger .357?" The detective's tone turned more serious as he searched Nick's face for an answer.

"Detective, what are you doing here? And what's with the attitude? I'm no rookie. So how about giving it to me straight."

The detective set the notepad down on his lap, still propped open. He took a deep breath and exhaled.

"Mr. Pajak, sir, I'm sorry to inform you that your ex-wife," glancing down, he read, "Ms. Stephanie Pajak, has been found dead." He paused, allowing the information to sink in. "We're not sure what happened, as yet. A suicide note was discovered at the scene. But we haven't ruled out foul play."

Nick's mouth slivered open, taking in a sharp breath. His eyes became vacant. Exhaling, he forced the air between his lips. For several seconds he felt as if his heart had stopped beating.

"Again, sir, I'm truly sorry." The detective spoke with sympathy.

Nick stood up and stepped away from his chair. He went to the sliding glass door that led to the backyard, his head held high, eyes forward. Detective Sherman also stood and placed his notepad on the coffee table. He walked to the opposite side of the room, eyeing Nick, evaluating his reaction.

Nick remained stoic, staring off into the dark backyard, his back to the detective. He brought his hands up to his eyes, and then ran them through his hair as he murmured inaudibly, "How'd she die?"

"Excuse me, sir?" the detective said.

"I said, how did she die?" Nick turned to meet the judgment from across the room.

"She was shot, in the face."

"That son of a bitch. I knew it. Damn you, Stephanie. Why didn't you listen?" Nick brushed away tears from his cheeks.

"Who are you talking about?"

"Russell Lynch, her boyfriend, that piece of trailer-park trash."

"Who?"

"Oh, Detective, don't go there. I've played this game plenty of times. And you know full well who she lived with and who he is." Nick's eyes narrowed, revealing a loathing for the younger man.

The air in the room suddenly felt stale and thick.

"Mr. Pajak, she was killed with a gun that was registered to you, your Ruger .357."

Nick went expressionless. He walked back to his chair and flopped into it, his eyes bloodshot, blinking wetly.

Caught in the undertow of Stephanie.

Twenty=four

A minute or two passed. Streams of tears coated Nick's cheeks; his nose was red. Detective Sherman went back to the couch, sat down, and discreetly pretended to be engrossed in his notepad.

"If you don't mind, sir, a few more questions," the detective said as he perused his notes. "Mr. Pajak, you were recently in Las Vegas. What took you there?"

"Ah, yesterday . . . ?" He looked over at the detective. "Yeah, yesterday."

"And what brought you there?"

"What?" said Nick, still in a fog.

"Please, Mr. Pajak, as you implied, you know the drill. Start from when you first arrived in Las Vegas and tell me about the day."

"Hold on. I need a minute."

"I'm only doing my job, sir."

"Uh-huh." He adjusted himself in the chair, crossing his left leg away from the detective, and crossed his arms. Nick composed himself. "I had an early-morning flight to Vegas, as you already know. Got there about nine fifteen, rented a car, and went to the office. I met with Joe, my business partner, signed tax returns and a couple of other documents, then had lunch with Stephanie, and got back to the office around three p.m. Later, I had dinner with Joe and his wife and caught the last flight back. It was about eleven thirty p.m. by the time I walked in the door. That's it."

"Lunch . . . just the two of you? And where did you eat?"

"We met at the Hot & Juicy Crayfish restaurant off Spring Mountain Road." Something suddenly broke inside Nick. His voice began to rise.

"You want to know how many goddamn crawdads I ate too? Oh, I'd say about fifty. She had the king crab legs, maybe three or four in the—"

"Please, sir," Detective Sherman interjected. He deliberately paused, looking away, then down at his notepad before continuing. "And you met with her for what purpose? What did you talk about?"

"Oh, you're a real piece of work." Nick's lips tightened, and then as suddenly, he relaxed. *Calm down. Simply cooperate,* he thought. *Behaving like an ass isn't going to bring her back.*

Intellectually, he knew there was a difference between being the person asking the questions and the one answering them, especially under duress. He would have imagined he'd react better—with professionalism, given his experience. Now he felt anything but professional. Nick took another moment to settle himself.

"All right," he exhaled loudly. "Whenever I'm in town I'll call up Stephanie and we'll have lunch, dinner, whatever. We may not be married anymore, but I can assure you, I always had her best interest at heart. She was a big part of my life for a long time."

Detective Sherman nodded, noticing the change in Nick's attitude. "And what did you two talk about? Anything you can remember would be a big help."

"The normal stuff: what she'd been up to, was she still seeing Russell, work, that sort of thing." Nick hesitated, "Honestly, she looked tired."

"What do you mean?"

"Tired, like she hadn't been sleeping. Dark rings under her eyes."

Nick hadn't been completely forthright with the detective. He looked across the room in a haze, revisiting her many bouts of alcoholism. Feeling compelled to protect Stephanie's memory, he revealed nothing private to the detective.

"Are you aware of her doing any drugs?"

"No. Not aware of any drugs."

"Did you two argue about anything?"

"No. Everything was good."

"Did she ask for anything? Money?"

"Is this really necessary?"

Detective Sherman gave Nick the *detective* frown.

"Sure, I gave her a few bucks."

Detective Sherman jotted down the information, then stood up, and put the notepad away in his left chest blazer pocket. He walked around the coffee table, stopping to touch a picture of Nick's sister, Shannon, and her family, hanging on the wall. He turned back to Nick and pulled out his pad again.

"Your girlfriend, Mary, what's her last name?"

"Berean."

"Please, spell it out for me."

"B-e-r-e-a-n," Nick spoke slowly, becoming more agitated. For a split second, he thought of the possibility of Mary somehow being involved, and then as suddenly, it was gone.

"Has she ever met the deceased before? Any history between the two?"

The detective's line of questions, and bringing Mary into the exchange, was enough for Nick. He had always been an outstanding detective. He leaned forward, tilting his head awkwardly at the man towering a few feet away.

"Dave—no bullshit—I know why you're here. Just ask me." Nick's voice was steady and emotionally detached.

"This is my job." Detective Sherman looked down at his shoes. "They thought it might be easier if I broke the news to you in person."

"Bullshit," Nick said calmly. He took in a deep breath, "I didn't touch her. And specifically, who are *they*?"

"Uh . . ."

"Uh-huh, cut the crap, Dave. I'm not your guy, and you know it. You already know who the real perp is. Don't you?"

"Look, Mr. Pajak, you have to admit there are a whole lot of coincidences. You were in Vegas yesterday, you had lunch with the victim, and—"

"Stop! You're talking about a person here. Use her real name."

"You're right, I apologize." Detective Sherman took a moment to reassemble his thought process. "You and Ms. Pajak were seen together having lunch. Less than fourteen hours later, she was found dead, shot in the face with a gun registered to you. As you are well aware, it's very rare for a woman to commit suicide by this method. And—"

"And you're absolutely right. That's the *exact* reason why I'm eliminated as a suspect. There's no possible way I would have shot her in the face, and then leave a suicide note. That's much too sloppy. This is obviously a crime of passion."

"You also took the last flight out last night. You have to admit there are quite a few facts pointing in your direction."

"Again, you're right. Then answer me this, what's my motive? How exactly do I benefit from her death? Have you given *that* any thought?"

The detective didn't answer.

"I'll tell you what, Mirandize me and take me in, because I'm not saying another word. But I guarantee I'll mop the floor with you and the department over this."

The detective leaned against the wall, crossing his arms, seeming to consider his options.

Nick continued. "You've seen how our chicken-ass judicial system works. Go ahead, Dave, make your decision. I'm waiting."

The detective made a few more entries into his notepad.

"The department has yet to determine your level of involvement, if any. I'll be back in touch if we have any further questions."

"Then we're finished here?" Nick asked.

The detective nodded and said, "Sir, again, I am really sorry for your loss."

"Then you should leave," Nick said, disregarding the detective's halfhearted apology.

"I understand."

Under his breath, Nick muttered, "No, you really don't."

Detective Sherman made his own way out. Nick stayed in his chair. Tears fell for Stephanie, his last for her.

* * * * * *

MARY SAT AT home, consumed with worry. Eventually, she fell asleep on the couch, a throw blanket covering her legs.

Darkness had won the night.

Twenty-five

Nick pounded hard on the front door. The sound echoed throughout the neighborhood like firecrackers a night after the Fourth of July. Dogs barked.

"Mary, I know you're in there." Nick's voice pierced the night's chill.

The hallway light flickered on, and then her figure passed in front of the door's glass panes. The porch light came on, the door opened slightly, an inch or three, revealing Mary's peering eye. When she saw Nick was alone, she opened the door the rest of the way. Standing back, keeping her distance, her face was sad, her hair disheveled.

She wore a dark blue, satin pajama top that reached the tops of her thighs. Nick noticed her tanned legs, but it was her feet that stole his attention. They were clad in a pair of lime-green slippers with brown spots, a fringe of white lace encircled the opening, and large red frogs' tongues hung over her toes. Certainly, the ugliest pair of slippers he had ever seen.

"Are you okay?" she asked, appearing confused. "What time is it?"

Nick's temporary lapse of focus had an unexpected calming effect, though short-lived. In a firm voice he said, "How did you know?"

"Know what?" Mary rubbed the sleep from her eyes.

"How did you know something bad was going to happen?" His tone rose unexpectedly.

"Oh, Nicky, darling . . . So, you believe me now?"

"No, I don't! And don't give me any more of that black dream crap." Anger, doubt filled his mind.

"Not so loud," she said, gesturing for him to lower his voice. "And I really don't like this side of you."

"Well, it's not every day your ex-wife is murdered. So, please excuse my damn delivery."

"What? Murdered? Who?"

"Stephanie!"

"Oh, dear God," Mary brought her hands up to her mouth. "The police officer didn't tell me anything. Nicky, I'm— I'm . . ." Her eyes instantly began to well up. She grabbed his arm, pulling him inside. "Sorry."

THEY SAT ON her couch and talked for hours. For the first time in Nick's life, as much as he could, he opened up. His eyes reddened as he spoke of Stephanie and their old life together. He recalled their better days of love and laughter: how she tolerated his passion for camping, fishing, and the great outdoors. Stephanie was more of a Ritz-Carlton type of girl, preferring massages to air mattresses and filet mignon to beans and franks cooked over an open fire.

It was early morning when Nick finally shared the heartbreak of how Stephanie had left him, about what she said to her friends, that "Sometimes love alone isn't enough." The entire time, he remained stone-faced, voice unwavering, giving little hint of emotion, not a single tear spilling down his cheek. Meanwhile, Mary wept, lying in his lap, clutching his legs, feeling his pain for him. She understood his brokenness.

Nick left before Mary's tears began to dry, fearing his own words. Neither made more mention of her dream. While driving home he prayed for numbness. His feelings were much too close to the surface, and functioning in that state had never worked for him. He needed sleep.

Forcing away a nightmare—
If you don't talk about it, you'll forget about it soon enough.

Part 3

Twenty=six

Love . . . can push a man out of character. It can compel him to do things he swore he would never do. Once set in motion, loves leaves nothing untouched.

WHEN HE WAS a child, Nick and his family had often spent Sunday afternoons at the "Horsey Swing-Swing Park," better known as Irvine Regional Park. It had been Orange County's first official park, with 477 acres, visited by thousands of people a year. There was nothing better than spending the day playing Frisbee, eating charcoal-grilled hot dogs, climbing one of the many sycamore trees, or tossing around a football. And on those special days, a pony ride—always Dad's treat. Even though the ponies only trudged around in a circle, the park held a special place in Nick's heart. It was the perfect setting for fall, and *his* Mary.

SYCAMORE AND OAK leaves flew upward in the late-afternoon breeze. The large ones, six to nine inches long, hung in the air, momentarily freed from gravity, before gently floating down to the ground.

The leaves crumpled under Nick and Mary as they play-wrestled. Nick had the advantage of superior strength and weight, and he chose to deploy the highly effective "armpit tickle" technique. With one hand, he held both of Mary's arms over her head against the ground. Then he lightly touched her exposed underarms using his fingers to flit and dance across her exposed skin. She squirmed against him, crying out for him to stop.

"Okay, okay . . . you win." Mary's lips tightened in between the laughter and shrieks. "No, seriously, Nick, stop. I'm gonna . . . stop!" Her head rocked back and forth as she tried with all her might to free a shoulder and shake him off.

"Then say it."

"Yeah, yeah, anything. Please, stop. I can't breathe."

Nick relinquished his grip and carefully rolled off her. He kept his eyes on her, believing retaliation would soon be at hand. There was none.

Mary lay breathing heavily. She smiled and actually giggled as she gazed up at the smattering of white clouds above.

"Yes, it's true, Nicky. I'm totally, undeniably, unflappably, and any other *un-* word in love with you." Rolling onto her side, she faced Nick, and tenderly added. "I do love you, too much."

He longed to hear those words again. After he had last seen her, early that Sunday morning, he had flown back to Las Vegas, where he'd spent the next eight days handling Stephanie's funeral and personal affairs. Nick was the last of her family. Mary did not join him. She said it was an issue he had to handle alone.

During that week, Russell Lynch, Stephanie's on-again, off-again boyfriend and convicted drug felon, was arrested in New Mexico. According to the news reports, Lynch had evaded the law for four days until he was detained while hiding in a friend's basement. It was the friend who had called the police after seeing Lynch's profile on television. Lynch later was transferred to Las Vegas where he was charged with murder. The press conjectured that Lynch was high on meth when he shot and killed Stephanie.

As a courtesy, Detective Sherman contacted Nick to tell him about the arrest before it hit the news. Nick watched every second of coverage. He was relieved that the killer had been apprehended, but he knew that it was only the beginning. Still, it gave him a sense of closure.

Nick leaned over and kissed Mary. His lips quivered nervously.

"Remember that night, at my house, before that whole police business?" Nick asked.

Mary sat up, grabbing her knees. Nick sat up too.

"Sure, you made a great dinner for me."

"Thanks, but that's not what I meant. Do you remember my poem?"

"Of course I remember, at least the part you read. Then we were so rudely interrupted by your buddy from Las Vegas," Mary said sarcastically.

Nick pulled the wrinkled envelope from his back pocket.

"There's something I wanted to say before you read this. Uh . . . I . . . "

Nick held the envelope enticingly in front of Mary.

"Oh, hush and give it to me."

Mary snatched the envelope from his hand, surprising him by having such fast reflexes. Just as quickly, she opened the envelope and pulled out the single sheet of paper.

"Hmmm. Now what do we have here?" Mary said.

Beads of sweat sprang up along Nick's hairline. He gazed blankly off into the distance.

"Mary, I hope you know how I feel . . . about you."

As she unfolded the bottom of the page, her eyes immediately came to rest on the last sentence.

"And I wanted to ask you—"

Mary leaped over, knocking Nick sideways as she landed on top of him.

"Yes. Yes, oh yes," Mary said through shimmering eyes.

Their combined weight crushed the leaves beneath Nick, releasing a pungent odor of sycamore musk. The poem, discarded in the midst of Mary's excitement, ended up five feet away on a greener section of lawn. The bottom of the sheet flapped in the light breeze, revealing *the question* Nick had added that morning.

Walking in Love.

Twenty-seven

Mary's head rested on his chest, her hand roamed over his stomach, moving in and out of his shirt. Her excitement had settled into a joyous contentment.

"What about next summer?" Nick suggested.

"Really?" Mary smiled. "I would love that," she said calmly, although her fingers began to twitch.

"I know you've only had a few seconds to think about it, but any preferences to a month or day?" he asked.

"Yeah." Mary slapped Nick on his forearm and rolled off to sit up. "It's only the most important day in a woman's life. So, absolutely."

Nick also sat upward. He gazed into her eyes.

"You trust me, right?"

"Sure do, but only with my heart," Mary giggled.

"Then close your eyes and I want you to listen."

"Nick, what are you up to now?"

"I've got something in mind. Please close your eyes." He motioned his hands over her eyes. "Have a little faith."

Mary sat, right leg over her left, her back straight in perfect posture; she blinked, and then shut her eyes.

"Nicky, I'm doing this with the understanding it's because I love you. And if you think you can sweet-talk me . . . Okay, maybe you can—"

"Shhh," Nick whistled.

"Sorry."

There was silence for a time. Mary's eyes remained closed, without expectation. Nick moved to her side and looked intently at her profile. First, at her face, tanned from the summer—she had a perfect petite nose and flawless skin. Her lips were full and red, flowing with excitement. One of the straps of her light summer dress had slipped off her shoulder. The way she sat, with her breasts thrust out; the thin fabric scarcely covered her protruding nipples. He had to stare.

Nick quickly pulled an engagement ring out from his pocket and repositioned himself in front of her. He gently touched her arm, and slid his hand down to her wrist and hand.

"Do you hear that?" he asked, stroking the back of her hand.

"You mean the birds?"

"Well, that's one. Anything else?"

Mary turned her hand over, grasping his.

"All I hear are birds."

Nick brought her hand up to his chest. "How about now?"

She opened her eyes and looked directly into his.

"Darling, what are you doing? There's no need for any of this. I already have all that I want. You're just trying to make me cry, aren't you? Can't—"

"Shhh. Close your eyes. . . . What else do you hear?"

She shut her eyes and a tear broke free. Noticing, Nick extended her left hand and quickly placed the ring on her finger.

Instantly, her eyes opened, and she looked down at her hand.

"No . . . oh wow." Her breath rushed out.

She brought the sparkler closer. The two-carat diamond set in white gold shimmered in the sunlight. Mary began to shake.

"I don't . . . It's gorgeous." Her words sounded jumbled.

She looked lovingly into his eyes, leaned forward, and kissed him with purpose. Her hands swung around to the back of his head, caressing his hair. Her lips were ripe with desire. Nick could feel her weight pressing against him. Excitement filled his body.

After one last celebratory kiss, Mary rotated around so she was in between his legs. She leaned back against him. Nick, behind, noticed her hands were still shaking. He scooted closer and wrapped his arms around her chest and shoulders. He could feel her heart. It was pounding hard and fast.

Mary lifted and tilted her left hand back and forth, fixated on the ring's reflecting rainbow colors.

"Well, it's about time. Shame on you for making me wait," Mary said.

Nick laughed.

Mary giggled.

It had always been Nick's plan to avoid the traditional getting down on one knee thing. He had done that with Stephanie, and Mary was no Stephanie. She was more.

Later that night, they made love for the first time.

* * * * * *

NICK'S FIRST CALL was to his mom. Fascinating how, even as adults, men seek the approval of their mothers. As for Momma Pajak, she was thrilled for him. Having never remarried herself, she did express concern that it might be a bit soon, especially in the wake of Stephanie's death. Nick's reply was short and sincere, "Mom, love doesn't follow a calendar. I'm in love with her." Nevertheless, Momma Pajak was ecstatic at the thought of another woman wanting to share her son's life.

His next calls were to his two sisters, and then finally, to Dad. Everyone wanted to meet the woman who had stolen Nick's heart. His original thought had been to hold off on the whole family circus until he had everything in order. But as mothers do, Momma Pajak had another plan. What could be better than a family reunion and introduction of her Nicholas's fiancée?

How could life ever be the same?

Twenty-eight

Two weeks later, the Pajak bunch started arriving in waves. Momma Pajak pulled in first, wanting to get the pulse of her beloved Nicholas. Sister Shannon, her husband Jesse, and their three kids flew in from Atlanta. Pam, the youngest Pajak and forever single, drove down the coast from San Francisco. Even Dad, with his fourth bride, twenty-eight-year-old Chilean Veronica, showed up. Dad and Veronica stayed at the local hotel. Probably best since Momma Pajak, who would never admit to it, couldn't stand Veronica. Nick's home overflowed with the rest of the family.

Pam knocked three times on the kitchen table, quickly placing her cards facedown.

"Ugh, who knocked?" Shannon showed her displeasure.

"Your lovely sister," said Nick, "the one sitting there . . . looking a little *too* innocent."

Pam snickered. Nick picked up a card from the top of the deck: two of diamonds. He tossed it on the discard pile.

Mary leaned on Nick and whispered, "What's a knock again?"

"It means you get one last card, and then we turn them over to see who the loser is. Remember, you count only the same-suited cards."

"Oh yeah, got it. Thanks." She straightened herself up, eyeing the two of diamonds. "Nope, I'll take my chances," and picked the next card on the stack. The Queen of Diamonds. She beamed. "Look, Nicky," she said, excitedly bouncing in her chair. "Is this it?"

Nick took a glance at her hand. "Well, put it down."

Pam laughed, "Why, yes, Nicky, look."

Mary placed the ten, Queen, and Ace of Diamonds on the table. "Thirty-one," she exclaimed.

"Oh shit. Scat," Shannon called out. "See, Pam, if you didn't knock, she never would have gotten that card. Nice start."

"So, I win?" Mary looked at Nick.

He nodded with a wink. "That hand."

Momma Pajak approached from the kitchen, carrying chips and a bowl of salsa. "What I'd miss?"

"Little Miss Knock-Happy over there," Shannon screamed with sarcasm, "couldn't keep her fist off the table, and we all lost."

"Beginner's luck," Pam chimed in.

"Now, girls, let's keep a civil tongue. We don't want to give Mary the wrong impression about us." Momma Pajak touched Mary's shoulder. "Why don't you two come out back, and we could have a little chat." She looked at Nick. "Nicholas."

"Oooh, Nicky, you get to have a little chat with the mom," Pam laughed.

"Come on, Mom, we're right in the middle of a game," Shannon said, revealing her competitive side.

"Honey, I would like to speak to them before your father and his wife return. You know how he is."

Nick rolled his eyes.

"Absolutely, Mrs. Pajak. This could be fun," said Mary.

Pam mouthed at Nick, "This could be fun," and smiled.

Nick smirked at Pam and boldly stated, "She can hold her own. Your turn is coming."

* * * * *

A MATURE ORANGE tree arched its branches, providing ample shade for the three sitting on the back patio. With Jesse at the park with the kids and Dad and his Latina bombshell at the hotel, it gave Momma Pajak an opportunity to have one-on-two time with the couple.

"Honey, may I take a closer look at your ring?" Momma Pajak asked.

Mary, unabashed, reached across the table. "It's so beautiful. And Nick made me wait for it too."

"Oh my. The diamond is quite large."

"I know, more than I ever expected. And I would have been happy with a simple band. It didn't have to be gold either." The cadence of her speech accelerated. "He's really very romantic. I should tell you how he asked me."

Nick touched her knee, and she instantly stopped talking.

Recomposed, Mary continued more slowly, "Nicky, maybe you should tell your mother how you proposed to me."

"I asked. She said yes, and I gave her the ring." Nick appeared every part of being uncomfortable.

Mary looked at him lovingly, giggled, and smiled. "You can be so silly at times." She changed her focus to Momma Pajak. "I just love that about him."

"We all do." Momma Pajak laughed, letting the story go, knowing it would be told countless times before the weekend would end. She had her own agenda.

"Mary, dear, please tell me about your family. Nick mentioned something about a brother?"

Mary squirmed in her chair. Nick's ears perked up.

"I have a brother . . . Kent. He can be quite wonderful . . . at times. But, right now is not one of those." She turned to Nick, "Sorry, they can't make it. He gave me some stupid excuse, so I stopped listening. I'm pretty mad at him right now."

Nick raised his eyebrows, his mind churning on this new information.

"That's a shame we won't be able to meet him," Momma Pajak half smiled. "Perhaps on my next trip?"

"Definitely." Mary paused. "Well, here's a thought—Maybe if you could stay a couple of days longer, I'm sure I could set something else up. You're going to love his wife, Angie."

Nick grimaced. The idea of having the family stick around for an extra day or two didn't thrill him.

Momma Pajak took in Nick's expression. "Mary, that's very kind of you. But unfortunately, I don't think this time around is best for everyone. I believe Pam works on Tuesday. And Shannon and the kids are going down to San Diego for a few days of vacation. They may here be under the pretext of a family reunion and meeting you, but anytime she can get to Southern California, she takes every advantage of it. As to Nick's father and what his new bride's plans are, you'll have to ask them."

"Okay, then next time. You could even stay with me."

"We'll see." Momma Pajak took a long pause. "I understand you were married before. How long were you married?"

Mary looked at Nick as if he had given up one of their private secrets.

"I got married pretty young." Turning back to Momma Pajak, "It was one of those things where we weren't really a good match. He was from the Midwest, and I'm a home-grown California girl. I've been in Orange County most of my life. So, to answer your question, eleven years."

"Hello, hey, we're back and come bearing gifts. Where's that beautiful Mary of ours?" a voice came from inside the house.

Nick saw his dad with his hands full of boxed presents of sundry sizes and shapes. Veronica carried in one small box. Her purse slipped off her shoulder as she stepped down onto the backyard patio.

"Mary, these are for you. And if I didn't say it before, welcome to the family." Nick's dad placed the stack of gifts in front of Mary. Veronica topped the pyramid with the last of the packages.

Momma Pajak cringed.

As only Dad would have it, all seven presents were marked with Mary's name alone. He loved to share his abundance, especially with beautiful women.

Shut the shutters, they can see in.

Twenty=nine

Nick had anticipated the onslaught of chaos. He had already been hit with a barrage of questions. The kind only family could get away with, especially in that area he didn't care to explore—feelings. Life always offers up choices . . . and ways to escape.

AT EXACTLY SEVEN twenty-one Saturday morning, he snuck out of the house, leaving Momma Pajak and the rest of the clan sleeping. His cell phone lay conspicuously on the kitchen table with a yellow Post-It note on top. The note read:

> *Free day for everyone. Be back tonight.*
> *—Love, Nick*

After picking up Mary, he drove south. Their destination: Laguna Beach, a quaint coastal town of about 24,000, and one of Orange County's oldest cities, world-renowned for its scenic sunsets. Mary seemed to like going there, though Nick thought of it as more of an artsy-fartsy community, not what he was into. Yet, being away from the family's bedlam and pleasing Mary at the same time made it a win-win scenario.

Mary was unusually quiet, but judging by her smile, she was delighted by the spontaneous outing. She rolled down her window, allowing the cool breeze to tousle her hair. Nick made no mention of the previous day with his family. He offered no excuses for Mom's questioning or Dad's lavish display of his wealth.

They had breakfast at one of Laguna's better-known eateries, The Cliff Restaurant.

While they waited for their omelets, Mary said, "Nicky, about next summer." She took a sip of coffee. "I've got the date."

Nick's eyebrows rose.

"How about June?"

"For?"

"Our wedding."

"Sounds fine," he responded nonchalantly, looking out on to the ocean view.

"Fine? . . . Okay, then how's June 18th? Does that sound fine too?"

"Sweetie, you can pick any date you like. It really doesn't matter to me. The month, the day, the time—they're irrelevant."

"So, I could pick any day . . . and you don't care, because it's all irrelevant to you?" Mary suddenly became loud.

"Mary," he paused, and then in a lower tone, "let me tell you what I do consider relevant. I will be there, on whatever day you want, dressed in whatever you want me to wear. It could be a huge church wedding with the entire congregation present or down the street at the local courthouse with only the two of us. Just as long as I can spend the rest of my life with you—nothing else matters. Then, yes, the specifics are all irrelevant to me. But as to you, never."

Mary's eyes widened. "Aren't you the sweetest man! I don't know how you do it, but you surprise me every time."

She got up, went around the table, and kissed him squarely, hands cradling his chin. Other patrons looked on, enjoying their moment.

"Speaking of surprises," Nick said, "I got something I wanted to talk to you about that's kinda interesting."

"Oh, there's more? Well, aren't I having the best day?"

"Actually, this involves your brother."

Mary took the seat next to him. "Yeah?" Her smile softened.

"Joe called real early this morning. You remember me telling about my business partner, right?"

"Uh-huh?"

"I had him do a little digging around on Opal to see if he could come up with anything. Well, he did."

Mary's focus intensified. "And?"

"I can't say with absolute certainty, but according to Joe, it could change your family's composition."

"No!"

"All the dates fit, and he seems confident."

Mary exhaled. It was one of the rare occasions when she was rendered speechless.

Nick continued, "The big question is for you. I need to know what you want me to do. Would you like me to continue on, in a formal investigation mode or stop here? Keep in mind that what we discover may not be pretty; it hardly ever is."

"I don't know." She looked blank. "Huh. I'm not sure what to do." She paused. "I guess you're not going to tell me what Joe said, are you?"

"Sorry, not at the moment. In the meantime, how about you sit on it a few days and let me know what you would like me to do."

"I've got some time to think about it?"

"As long as you like."

He was glad Mary hadn't pressed the issue. He felt awkward enough not being completely forthright with her, though he had given her a huge clue. Joe had called five minutes before he left that morning. "Mary has a niece," were Joe's first words, followed by, "and I have the proof." Their call was brief, and Nick had very few details.

* * * * * *

AFTER BREAKFAST, THEY took a long walk through the downtown shopping area. She bought two T-shirts, and they shared a chocolate ice-cream cone along the boardwalk.

Later, they traveled inland for a tethered balloon ride at the Great Park in Irvine. Many of the locals called it "The Big Pumpkin in the sky" because of its bright orange color and shape.

As the sun went down, they drove back to Mary's. After a light meal of homemade bruschetta and a little white wine, they curled up together on the sofa. It was the textbook ending to a perfect day.

By the time Nick walked in through his garage door it was almost midnight. Everything was as he had left it: Momma Pajak, Shannon and Jesse asleep in their beds, the kids and Pam snuggled up on the pullout couch and blowup mattresses in the living room. His cell phone appeared to have been left untouched on the table. He grinned at the silence.

Boy, if these walls could talk. I'm sure Dad had a few choice words for me today.

Nick's smile broadened.

He knew in the morning he'd have some explaining to do, but now he was prepared for the family. They would forgive him—that's what family does.

All they would have to do was look into his eyes.

Thirty

As expected, Mary was a huge hit. Momma Pajak fell in love with Mary's confidence, while Dad donned his finest charismatic efforts to impress her. Mary happily bounced from one family member to the next, showing off the engagement ring to smiles all around. She listened attentively to everyone's stories about Nick. Even Shannon, who was notorious for telling it like it is, pulled Nick off to the side, confiding that Mary was a catch.

When the family extravaganza finally left town, Nick was exhausted. Yet he made the time so they could be in each other's arms. The following morning the bombardment of phone calls started. Each family member took it upon themselves to give their stamp of approval. Nick's favorite comment came from his sister Pam. She said, "I'm glad to see you're marrying up this time." He wasn't sure if she was joking.

Mary laughed at his unease as he tried to explain Pam's comment.

"Oh, pay no attention, Nicky. They're all happy for you. But, you do have to admit they're right. Look at me. I'm pretty awesome, witty, and obviously, no one can resist my charm."

"You're a princess, all right," Nick smirked. "There's no denying that."

"Then you're admitting it, I *am* a princess. So then, I'm worth the biggest, most expensive, elaborate wedding there is. Yeah, I did say *expensive*, didn't I?"

"Uh-huh."

"I can see it now, rolling up to the church in a horse-drawn carriage. Thousands of my fans are screaming and yelling for the merest acknowledgment from me. I do the princess wave—they go wild."

"I can see none of this has gone to your head."

Mary laughed.

"Okay, do another. Tell me again what your dad said."

"This is the last time. Dad thinks you're a babe."

"Yeeesss." Mary gave a victory fist pump.

"Are you finished?" Nick asked.

"Nicky, I love you."

"What am I going to do with you?"

"Only keep loving me, darling." Mary batted her eyelids.

"That's the easy part."

"Opal had a baby. I'm right, aren't I?"

Nick frowned. "Whoa. How did you get from 'I love you' to 'Opal had a baby'?"

"I can read people too, especially you, big boy." She pointed and poked Nick's shoulder. "I want the full investigation on Opal and this alleged baby of hers. I do have my doubts.

However, if there is any chance her child is family, I'll need every available piece of information in hand before bringing it to my brother."

Mary had no idea of the lengths and the expense Nick had already gone to, to fulfill her request in advance.

A "Thank you" breath passed through him.

Part 4

Thirty-one

Blurred Edges . . .

SEVERAL MONTHS PASSED and winter came. The happy couple's relationship grew closer, dependent, filled with the joy of being in love. They agreed on a wedding date, June 18th, Grandmama Matos's birthday. Nick thought the day should be about them as a couple, but he didn't put up much of a fight. After all, Mary was all he wanted.

They celebrated a quiet Christmas together, in front of Nick's fireplace. Momma Pajak expressed disappointment that Nick had chosen to stay in California for the holidays. Frankly, she seemed more upset about Mary not coming out than anything else. She told Nick he was never very good at sharing. They laughed.

Nick and Mary had agreed that they wouldn't exchange gifts. Instead, they were to make cards for each other. She honored their arrangement and looked understandably distraught when Nick brought out a present bearing her name. That was, until she unwrapped the bottle of Mr. Bubbles. She smiled suggestively.

Nick had engineered their gift-free pact for a reason. He needed more time. By the middle of January, it had come together.

As per Mary's request, The Papa & Pajak Detective Agency had completed its workup. It included individual background checks on each member of Opal's immediate family, their education, workplaces, and residences, with corroborating dates. The list of private details, sometimes obtained through not-entirely-legal means, was more explicit than Mary had bargained for. She came to realize that prying into someone else's life could be an unsettling experience. Then came the conclusive evidence: a copy of the girl's birth certificate, naming Kent Huffman as the father. Mary accepted the undeniable fact that a Miss Monika Grant was indeed her niece.

Nick suggested to Mary that she meet with Kent alone to give him the news. He felt it was a personal matter that he should stay out of. He had explained time and again that you can't sandbag people with information of this kind. Moreover, he hadn't met Kent yet.

Mary had her own thoughts.

* * * * * *

IT WAS SIX weeks later when Nick parked across the street from a house on Lake Mission Viejo. He glanced down, double-checked his watch and the address scribbled on his three-by-five notecard. His passenger, Monika Grant, looked past Nick to the Huffman residence. Her eyes widened, and her brows arched.

"Is that it?" Monika asked in a Texas drawl, clearly in awe.

The house was massive, contemporary in design, constructed of traditional building materials including reclaimed brick and cedarwood siding. The windows were classic French, multipaned, the frames heavily painted a glossy white. Stucco, a Californian staple, was nowhere to be found. The home's wood frame and shutters were artistically highlighted with a walnut shell color, and the sidings painted an almond latte. He estimated the home to about six thousand square feet and worth several million.

"Impressive, isn't it?" Nick remarked.

"Definitely. There aren't many homes like that in my neck of the woods." She paused, looking down. "Mr. Pajak, honestly . . . I'm more nervous than I thought I'd be. Maybe this wasn't such a good idea. It's not like he knows I'm coming."

Nick quickly turned to her as if he had anticipated her doubts. "I understand what you're feeling. It's like what we talked about before. All right, sure, it's going to be awkward at first. But it will work out fine."

"You sure?" She looked scared, even more so than that morning when Nick had picked her up at the airport.

"Positive."

He spoke with his usual self-assurance; chin high, hands steady, without the slightest quaver in his voice. In truth, he was just as nervous. He hadn't wanted to approach the situation in this manner.

She closed her eyes tightly, and by the way her mouth moved, appeared to be saying a prayer. After several moments, her anxiety seemed to lift. With a final deep breath, she said, "I'm ready now. Let's go."

"Mary's not here yet." He looked at his watch again. "Can you wait a little longer?"

"No. Y'all got me here, and I better do it now, or I'm not gonna do it at all."

Where are you Mary? he asked himself, looking at his watch again.

Nick got out of the car and opened the door for the younger woman. As they walked up to the house, he caught a glimpse of the body of water that lay beyond, Lake Mission Viejo.

"Gosh . . . huh," she mumbled, not realizing Nick could hear. Nick threw a reassuring hand on her shoulder, bringing a nervous smile to her face. They stepped up to the front door, looked for the doorbell, but there was none. Nick knocked on the oversized bronze doors.

They had walked right past the doorbell, which was some twenty feet behind them, located on the brick pillar marking the beginning of the front entryway.

They waited. Nick's palms were surprisingly dry. Monika took a step backward.

The door was opened by a man about six foot one, with blue eyes and thinning blond hair. Nick presumed him to be Kent. A few years older than himself, Kent was tanned, with a few wrinkles, and appeared to be in good shape for a man his age.

"Nick?" said the man.

"Mr. Huffman," Nick replied as they shook hands.

"It's finally nice to meet you," said Kent. "Mary told me you would be coming by."

"I hope this is a good time for you?" Nick stepped to the side, giving Monika the sign to move up.

"Sure, no problem at all. I see you brought company."

"Mr. Huffman, this is Monika Grant." Nick placed his hand on the small of Monika's back to nudge her forward.

Kent extended his hand, "Good to meet you, Monika," Kent unknowingly smiled. Monika greeted him with a two-handed shake.

"It's my pleasure, sir," Monika said, loosening her grip. She stared straight into his eyes, impressed by his gracious manners, considering that Kent had no idea who she was.

Kent returned her eye contact, not shying away. Nick looked on, studying their interaction. Finally, Kent disengaged himself, turning sideways.

"Well, come on in." Kent retreated backward as they entered. "And where's Mary?"

"She should be here any minute," Nick said with hope.

Kent led them through the foyer to a large family room. Monika's heels clicked, echoing off of the travertine floor and walls.

Monika sat next to Nick on one of three overstuffed couches. Kent sat some distance away, on the bench of a Steinway grand piano. The room was dominated by a huge fireplace that made the piano and couches look inconsequential. The walls were adorned with enormous paintings which appeared to be contemporary art. French doors at the far end of the room opened onto a breathtaking view of the lake.

Kent stared at the young woman.

Monika was an attractive woman whose personality did not give off the slightest hint she was aware of the power she held. Her skin was smooth and light-colored, setting off her brilliant light blue eyes framed by long lashes. She had three tiny moles on her neck, under her right ear. Her long, wavy blond hair complimented her features.

"Have we met before?" Kent asked, paying no attention to Nick.

"No, I don't think so." Monika nervously giggled like an anxious teen on a first date.

"You seem so familiar to me. Are you sure?"

"No, I'm certain."

Kent blinked, raised his eyebrows, and rubbed his temple. Turning to Nick, he continued, "I was surprised when Mary called, wanting to meet so urgently. What's this all about?"

"Actually, if you don't mind, I would like to wait for Mary. She should be here any moment."

"Huh? Okay."

There was a long pause.

Kent looked at Monika, "You have an accent. It's quite delightful. Where are you from?"

"Texas. I grew up in Dallas. Been there my whole life."

She tucked a few of her golden locks behind her left ear, revealing a small tattoo on the inside of her wrist—a heart, no color.

They heard the front door open.

"Hello? Kent? Nick?" Mary's voice reverberated.

"Down here in the fantasy room," Kent called out.

Mary walked into the room. She abruptly stopped and jerked backward, appearing suddenly vulnerable.

Nick and Monika rose in unison. Mary went up to Nick and kissed him, almost territorially.

"Mary, this is Monika," Nick said.

"Very nice to meet y'all," Monika said, extending her hand. "Nick speaks very highly of you."

"Thank you." Mary's eyes narrowed, and she crossed her arms.

"Mary," Nick said, touching her arm, "let's all take a seat. Perfect timing. I'm sure your brother is anxious to hear from you why we're here."

"No, I decided differently. I'm not going to do it." Mary waved her hands, indicating to Nick that he should proceed.

Everyone sat down, Monika on Nick's right and Mary to his left. Mary placed her hand on his thigh and forced a smile. An uncomfortable silence settled around them.

"Now that you're here," Kent spoke up, "Mary, what's the problem? How can I help you?"

Nick stared at Mary. She looked straight-ahead, all eyes on her. She didn't respond, staying close-lipped. Nick, feeling the pressure mount, stood up, reached into his pocket, pulled out the ring, and handed it to Kent.

Kent stared at it in the palm of his hand, seemingly dumbfounded. He closed his fingers over the ring, speechless. Monika looked on in anticipation.

"Is it yours?" Nick asked, already knowing the truth.

Kent didn't answer.

Mary bit her lower lip.

"Mr. Huffman?" Nick asked.

Finally, Kent said softly, "Yes. And no. It was mine . . . but I left it for her." Kent was visibly shaken. "It's always been hers. But, Nick, how?"

"There's more, sir. I can clear everything up. But first—"

"Hang on a sec." Kent appeared to be stewing over the ring's sudden reappearance. "This doesn't make any sense. You found it where? When?"

Nick blinked. "About eleven months ago."

"I left the ring on her grave, well—years ago. Lots of years ago."

Okay, this is getting weirder, Nick thought.

Monika stood up and blurted out, "Mr. Huffman, I'm your daughter. Opal Milton was my mom." She smiled nervously.

Kent looked up at her, tilted his head, and then nodded, clutching the ring.

"You're Opal's . . ." He stopped, rubbed his other hand over his mouth and chin. Kent slowly rose and took a few steps toward Monika. He stared into her eyes and swept her into a fierce hug.

"I *always* knew something wasn't right," he whispered.

Nick sat down next to Mary, watching them. He leaned over and, in a low voice, spoke into Mary's ear, "Looks like you made the right call. I was wrong."

Living half lives in different worlds.

Thirty=two

Over the next fifteen minutes, Nick recounted the events that had led to the discovery of Monika. Kent sat on the piano bench, Monika next to him, touching his arm now and then, as if in disbelief.

Treating it like a professional debriefing, Nick started at the beginning, with the finding of the ring. Something about it had stirred him, motivating him to return the golden object to its owner, regardless of the consequences. His instincts had been validated.

Nick had no explanation for the gap between when the ring was left and when he found it. He would think about that later.

He related the bizarre phone conversation with Mrs. Milton, Opal's mother and Monika's grandmother. This elicited a smirk from Kent. In fact, if it hadn't been for

Mrs. Milton accusing Nick of being Kent's coconspirator, Nick would never have found out his name. Mary did her part by unearthing Kent's yearbook dedication, and by doing so, confirmed the ring was her brother's because of the inscription.

Mary's amused expression grew tight and increasingly serious. She sat quietly as Nick recounted his actions, conversations, and private meetings, which she had no knowledge of. Inspired, he kept talking, oblivious to Mary's discomfort.

"Without Mary's help, we wouldn't be here today," he added.

Nick had taken advantage of the agency's resources, with Joe personally handling the investigation; they had little trouble coming up with the basic information on the Miltons.

"Our biggest break came from Opal's younger brother, Timmy. That's Uncle Tim to you," Nick shot a glance at Monika. "He remembered you, Kent, dating his sister back then. He recalled how Opal and his mother had argued over you—the long-haired surfer boy."

Kent scowled, "Yeah."

"According to Tim, the family up and moved to Dallas, and coincidentally, that was the end to the fighting. Tim said Opal seemed sad the entire time while they lived in Texas. She cried a lot, put on weight, and was sick most of the time. At one point, she wound up at the Baylor hospital in Dallas. The family never discussed Opal's ailments, although Tim had his own suspicions.

"He also talked about a more recent conversation you two had regarding Opal's death."

"That was quite a while ago," Kent said.

"Then, through the agency's connections, Joe managed to secure a copy of Monika's original birth certificate."

Monika sat next to Kent, listening in awe to the tale of Nick's journey.

Mary seemed shaken, her eyes widening despite knowing the outcome of the story. The intimate details may have been too much for her.

Monika spoke up. "My mom and dad, Michael and Bonnie Grant, told me at an early age that I was one of the few who were *chosen*. They never used the word 'adopted' with me. Dad found it impersonal and felt it didn't come close to conveying his true feelings about us."

"Yes, indeed, Monika, you were chosen—blessed," said Nick. She had been taken from the hospital that very morning. She had spent a lifetime in a God-fearing home where love swaddled her like a warm blanket. Of course, as a teenager, Monika experienced a few moments with her parents. But children grow up, become adults, and eventually embrace those very things they fought so hard against.

Kent appeared riveted. Monika nudged him occasionally, drifting ever closer.

Nick paused, taking in the friendliness between the two. He couldn't help but admire Kent. He was amazed that someone could be that accepting, with no more than a stranger's declaration: "Oh, by the way, you have a daughter, and here she is." Yet, he remained relaxed, almost as if he had been expecting it.

Nick picked up the story. "Finally, with the birth certificate in hand, it was only a few traceable steps to find Monika." He left out the details of the several day trips to the Las Vegas office and two longer ones to Dallas where he had first met with Monika.

Kent smiled and shook his head.

Monika leaned against Kent and spoke softly, "Y'all have missed much of my life because you had no idea. But now you know. I hope this is okay?" Her mouth quivered slightly.

Kent turned his head and whispered something to her.

Monika smiled and even exhaled a slight giggle.

Kent continued to speak privately, and then abruptly pulled back. First focusing on Nick, and then Mary, he said, "I want to thank you both. I'm speechless and not sure what to say right now. I always had a feeling . . ."

Kent didn't finish his sentence.

Seeing the emotion in Kent's face, Nick interceded, "You are very welcome."

The room fell quiet once more.

Gauging the awkwardness of the four of them sitting around looking at each other, Nick suggested that he and Mary leave for a couple of hours allowing Kent and Monika to get acquainted.

Nick looked at Mary. "Say about five o'clock?"

Mary didn't react.

"We're meeting up with Monika's uncles later on," Nick directed his comment to Kent.

Mary was expressionless, blank. Nick grabbed her hand and stood up, almost dragging her away.

Neither Kent nor Monika moved.

Dominos . . . tumble.

Thirty=three

⟡

Nick chauffeured Mary to Cook's Corner, a hole-in-the-wall biker bar a few miles from the Huffmans'.

Uncharacteristically, he rambled on about how great everything had turned out considering he had been there only to support Mary. Although he'd been unprepared to orchestrate the meeting, it had come off magnificently. Nick felt euphoric, describing the look on Kent's face when Monika revealed herself, how Kent had remained calm and cool, not even raising an eyebrow. Nick knew that look; he'd seen it in the mirror. But mainly, it was the ease with which Kent acknowledged Monika as his daughter. Most men's first instinct would be to jump to denial. Not Kent. He had literally welcomed her with open arms. Still, he wondered if Kent was harboring conflicted feelings. How would his wife and family take the news?

"I like your brother." *It was all worth it,* Nick thought.

Mary remained quiet, permitting Nick to revel in the moment.

At the restaurant, Nick headed straight to the bar. "Mary, what would you like? I want something special to celebrate." She gave no response. "Hey, how about a smile here? These are the good times."

"Water's fine," she said tepidly.

Nick picked up on her tone, knowing something was brewing from the instant she first walked into Kent's home.

"What's up, hon?"

"We need to talk."

"Oh, sure. You still want the water?"

"No," she said flatly.

Without ordering, Nick turned, gently took Mary's arm, and led her out to the patio area. He guided her past dining patrons, focusing on the furthest wooden picnic table sheltered in the shade of a sycamore tree. Nick sat on top of the table, feet up on the bench. Mary took a seat on the bench facing him, but not too close.

"What were you thinking?" she said. "What did you say to Kent about me? What did he tell you?"

"No, I tho—"

"And why were you sitting so close to her?" Her voice continued to rise. "I walk in, and she's almost in your lap. I wouldn't ever sit that close to another man in your presence—or ever. Is there something you to need to tell me?"

"Whoa, now, Mary, let's calm down." Nick reached over and touched her hand. She yanked it away.

"Okay . . ." Nick mumbled under his breath, slowly withdrawing his hand.

"What the hell do you mean by that?" Mary's anger continued to mount. "I don't have to calm down if I don't want to. You're not my fucking boss."

Nick was momentarily stunned, never having heard that type of profanity come out of her mouth before. He leaned back on his hands.

"Why didn't you wait for me? I wanted to be with you when you first met my brother. Really!" She shook her head. "And what did my brother say? I need to know. Tell me."

Nick leaned forward. "Is there anything else?"

"Yeah. I hate that you're so goddamned composed about everything. There's something seriously wrong with you."

"And?"

"And . . . stop that. I don't need a condescending attitude either."

"Uh-huh," Nick replied, not realizing he was smirking. Only fleeting, but it was enough that she caught a glimpse of it.

"Oh, and now you're laughing at me. I can't believe how fucking mad I am at you." Mary looked away, completely unraveled.

He waited; it was only a matter of time.

Mary started to cry, and then she sobbed.

He watched, expressionless, yet entirely confused. Experience had taught him to hold off on offering consolation at the first sight of a woman's tears. Most men tend to make that mistake—wanting to be the problem solver—forgetting they were the cause of it in the first place. And any attempt to comfort her now would be viewed as empty appeasement. Even so, he fought back the desire to hold her. If he was to wait a few minutes, letting the tears flow, she should become more receptive to an honest, open discussion.

After several minutes her tears, as calculated, subsided, Nick finally spoke.

"Mary, are you willing to talk about it now?"

Mary looked up, wiping away the last of the tears.

"Can you take me to my car?" She avoided eye contact.

"I would be happy to take you anywhere you like. But first, could you please look at me and let me know what's really going on here? You're crying, angry, and I haven't the slightest clue as to why. All I did was solve a puzzle, speak for you because you wouldn't, and most importantly, unite your brother with his daughter. I believe I've done everything you have asked of me, *and* more. Please, you've got to let me in."

Mary looked down at her hands. "Nick, I want to go. Please," she begged.

"Then, I take it we're through here."

"Yes, we are," Mary nodded.

SILENCE REIGNED DURING the drive back to the Huffman manor. When the car to came to a stop, Nick paused, wanting to broach the subject again. His hesitation gave her the break she sought. Mary jumped out of the car and made a beeline for hers. He had always opened the car door for her.

Nick quickly trailed.

"Wait, Mary. Give me a minute?"

He stopped in the middle of the street, watching while she slammed the car door and started the engine.

Mary looked ahead as if he didn't exist.

"Mary!" He yelled as she drove off, tires squealing. His hands dropped to his sides, his shoulders slumped.

Gravity pulls. Can love be so different?

Thirty-four

"Hey, Nick! Wasn't that Mary?" Kent's voice seemingly came out of nowhere.

Nick turned to see Kent and Monika walking toward him.

"Yeah, that was her," Nick said.

"Dude, my hat's off to you."

"What are you talking about?" Nick frowned.

"Listen, anyone who can handle my sister is a far better man than I am. As a matter of fact, you're about the only man I've ever seen come close to handling her. And from what she has told me, you're her kingpin."

"Kingpin? Yeah, right."

"Sure, she's a tough nut to crack. But don't let her occasional tantrum throw you for a loop. She says she loves you. And from the way she looks at you, it's obvious."

Monika remained in the background, pretending not to be listening.

Kent patted Nick on the back.

Nick was surprised at how much Kent knew of their relationship.

"Hey, since Mary's apparently not going with you tonight, would you mind if I tagged along with you and Monika when she meets her uncles? I would love to see how everyone's life turned out."

Monika stepped forward. Her eyes and smile inferred yes.

Upset, Nick impulsively blurted, "Kent, why don't you take her? You could probably use the time with her anyway."

"Are you sure?" Kent looked surprised.

"Yeah, positive. I'm sure you can handle it."

Nick briefly chuckled at the thought of Monika introducing Kent to everyone as her dad. His mind popped back to Mary, as always. At least now he was free to track her down and find out the real reasoning behind her irrational behavior.

"Great. Come on inside and give me the specifics," Kent said.

Nick gave Kent the addresses of Uncle Tim's house and Monika's hotel. The hotel was a good twenty miles out of Kent's way, but he was adamant about taxiing her there. Kent wore a grin that stretched across his face. Nick found him an easy man to read.

Before leaving, Nick gave Monika a reassuring hug and whispered, "Breathe in these moments."

"I will. And thank you so much . . . for everything." Monika hugged him harder.

After a few seconds, Nick released her. Monika clenched his hand. She looked into his eyes, and all of a sudden, she looked nervous.

"Don't forget, I'll pick you up tomorrow morning, ten sharp. Now, go and have a good time."

"All right." She scuffed her left foot backward. "I'll be ready. Promise." She seemed to want him to come with them, but also accepted why he wouldn't.

She let go of his hand. Nick smiled, turned, and walked away.

* * * * * *

DOWN THE ROAD, Nick's half smile faded as he realized he may have made a huge mistake.

Oh God, what did I do? I didn't even consider whether the uncles would've wanted to see Kent.

A car honked from behind. He hadn't noticed the light had turned green. He stepped on the gas.

Well, he's part of their family now . . . whether or not they like it.

He grinned and continued down the road.

Climbing the mountain yourself is the only way to earn it.

Thirty-five

By midnight, Nick had exhausted all avenues of communication. Mary hadn't returned any of his calls nor answered his butter-fingered texting efforts. Being old school, he preferred the phone to words on a screen.

The one call he did receive was from Monika. Nick gave a sigh of relief when she sounded happy saying, "Everything was *dandy*." She wanted to know if Kent could take her to the cemetery instead of him tomorrow. "Absolutely yes," Nick responded with certainty that it was now Kent's role to play, though he thought it polite of her to ask.

A HALF HOUR later, Nick stood on the step at Mary's front door, for the second time that night. It was dark inside, and he knew no one was home. He rang the doorbell anyway.

Where could she be?

He was worried. Nick believed society had a misperception about men and how they behave—well, sometimes. Often, men do worry about their loved ones. And then, the worry can build up so strong, it turns into fear. Fear is a man's worst enemy. It invariably results in him doing something stupid, including spewing hurtful words and irrational actions. Whatever the bad behavior—it's usually directly linked to his insecurity—the more insecure he feels, the more dreadful the behavior.

Nick didn't want to overreact. However, he was a man in love, and felt wounded for reasons he didn't quite understand. Sleep wouldn't come easy.

* * * * * *

THE NEXT MORNING, Nick woke up tired with tiny red eyes. He knew they would clear up after a quick shower and a shot or two of Visine. He distracted himself by reading the morning newspaper while sipping a coffee, and later he took a brisk walk around the neighborhood trying to get rid of the anxiety. He called Joe and updated him on the meeting between Kent and Monika. Joe too was emotionally vested in the case.

Having Kent take Monika to her uncle Tim's last night, and then to the cemetery that morning took the pressure off Nick. The task of driving Monika back to the airport was privilege enough for him.

Nick picked her up in front of her hotel. She wore a gray, body-hugging cashmere sweater over a blue blouse and white tank top. Her light flowing skirt completed her look. It seemed the less makeup she wore, the prettier she became. He opened the car door for her.

"I have so much to tell you," Monika said in haste as she handed Nick her bag. "Last night was wonderful. Everyone was so nice." She got into the car.

Nick shut her door, put the bag in the trunk, and went around to his side.

"Go ahead, give me all the details," he said while he buckled himself in.

"Uncle Timmy and his wife, Teri, I love them both. The second I walked in the door, they all made me feel right at home. Uncle Timmy"—her hands shook with excitement—"greeted me with a huge hug. And then when he saw Kent, holy macaloney, he pretty near ran me over to pull Kent in with us. The three of us just stood there holding each other."

Nick glanced over at her. She sat, all smiles. Her hands moved animatedly with every syllable she spoke.

"Then, I saw Uncle Timmy crying. The next thing I knew, tears were coming down my face. Ohhhh . . . Sorry about that." She peeked at Nick and tears fell. "I know how I can go on about such things."

Although focused on the road, Nick listened intently, his heart breaking a bit. Regret settled in with each of her words. He wished he had been there too.

"Then I met my other two uncles and their families. They all were quite amazing."

"Wow, that sounds . . . great. What about your grandparents, the Miltons? Were they there?"

Her hands dropped into her lap, and she became quiet.

"Don't worry, they'll come around," he said comfortingly.

"I hope so."

"One step at a time, Monika. Once the word gets back to them about how terrific you are, everyone in the family will be clamoring at your doorstep wanting to meet you. Have some faith."

"You're right," she smiled.

He asked nothing more. Those were *new* family issues she would eventually have to confront. He drove on, proud of what he had done to set things in motion.

NICK PULLED INTO the airport parking lot. After opening the car door for Monika, he felt her tug on his arm.

"Wait . . . before we go in, I need to ask you something."

Nick turned toward her.

"In y'all's world, I'm a nobody. Why me? . . . Why did you do all this?"

Nick's head drooped down—his eyes cried out that he didn't want to talk about it.

"Mr. Pajak," she said, not looking away. "Please, I've got to know."

Nick stood like a statue.

Unexpectedly, Monika's emotions erupted to the surface. She flew at Nick, hugging, crying, and pleading for answers.

Nick threw his arms around her, pulling her in tight.

"It's okay. I understand." Nick paused, allowing the tears to flow, whispering, "Listen, this one's for me."

Through wet eyes she asked, "What do y'all mean?"

Releasing her, he said, "After meeting you in Dallas, I had to help. And certainly for other reasons than I had originally intended. You see, I saw this beautiful, young woman starving for information about her biological parents. They were an absent piece in your world. You've probably been secretly carrying around the desire to find out anything and everything about them. I've seen that same hole in too many people's lives and not been able do anything about it. But with you, I could do something. Let's say it's my way of giving back, kinda like leveling the playing field for the good guys."

Monika held him hard.

After several seconds, she let go. Nick looked everywhere other than at her. He yearned for a cigarette, a cigar, or anything else that would distract his mind. He had long ago crossed over that line into caring.

Having the answer doesn't mean it's resolved.

Thirty-six

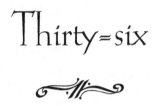

They stopped outside the doors to the main terminal at John Wayne Airport as others rushed past them. Monika pretended to smile. Her lower lip quivered for a brief moment. Her eyes were red.

"I'll be back soon," she said shakily. "Would it be all right if I called you? Maybe I can take you out to lunch."

She had about fifteen minutes before she had to be at her gate.

"Call me anytime," Nick said, although he would never let a woman buy him lunch. Some things were sacrosanct.

Monika grabbed his hand. He felt his heart drop.

"Thank you. I can never repay you for—"

"You're welcome, but please, it's time to get you in line." He released her hand and reached for her suitcase.

"Yeah, y'all are fit to be tied. I'm not about to let you off that easy. You are family now whether or not you marry Mary. And that means I get my say-so."

Nick released the suitcase and stood straight up, anticipating another emotional outpour. He had already expressed more than he thought he could.

"But, Monika, look how long the line is getting," he said, pointing inside the terminal.

"Oh, there's plenty of time. All I need is ten seconds."

"Uh-huh." Nick pursed his lips.

"Y'all have to hear this . . . for me."

Nick's chin drifted downward like a child anticipating a scolding. He blinked, feeling his own words were being turned back on him.

"Please," Monika took his face in her hands.

Nick acquiesced, staring into her baby blues.

"I've been fixin' to say this for some time. To thank you from my heart." She touched her heart. "Thank you for finding me, bringing me here, giving me another family. I can never repay you for your kindness."

She smiled, forcing a return smile out of Nick. "But mostly for taking the time to listen to me. For showing me about myself—who I am—for caring when you could have chosen not to. I love you, Mr. Pajak."

Monika pressed herself into his arms. Nick normally reciprocated with a quick hug from which he would then rapidly escape. But this time, he held Monika in his arms as if she were his own child. In a way, she was.

"I love you too."

Monika let go first and reached for her bag.

"I'll get that for you." Nick bent down to grab the luggage from her.

"No. I can take it from here."

You sure can, Nick thought.

"Thank you again. I'll be calling, soon."

She gave Nick a quick peck on the cheek and walked inside the terminal, quickly vanishing into the crowd. Nick stood smiling, happy—feeling.

* * * * * *

INVARIABLY, HE FOUND himself on Mary's front porch. He pressed the doorbell, hoping, waiting.

What would he say to her? Where had she been? Why was she so mad? Then it flashed into his mind.

Engagement jitters. That's it. Has to be.

He waited.

As he pressed the doorbell a third time, an old thought took hold.

Could this be Stephanie all over again? I can't handle any more empty picture frames.

The memories oozed out of him like from a tar pit, black and immobilizing. Doubt seeped in.

What if she doesn't love me anymore? Oh, God.

She wasn't home.

His song remained the same—discarded.

Thirty-seven

What was Nick to do? He could go to the nearest bar or to his local church. Both would serve him—one to mask the void, the other to fill it. In a reversal from drinking himself into oblivion, he chose neither. He had to be in his right mind when, and if, he next spoke to Mary.

He sat at the kitchen table staring into the nothingness. His left hand held up his chin like a pillar holding up a roof. In the past twenty-four hours he had been to her house three times and called at least a half-dozen times. Insecurities took their reserved places.

"Where are you?" he winced.

This is ridiculous. His mind needed at break. *You'll call me when you're ready.*

With that thought, Nick got up and went to the living room. He grabbed the remote control and dropped into the recliner. TV was a good choice; always had been, and there's no hangover. It carried him through the heartbreak of his divorce and the loneliness that followed. Within minutes, he was unconscious to the real world, immersed in someone else's problems. However, there was always the possibility that a single word or catchphrase could bring him crashing back to his own woes.

* * * * * *

HOURS LATER, AFTER the sun had gone down, his cell phone rang, pulling him out of his sleepy reverie.

"It's about time," he murmured, popping out of the chair. He had left his cell on the dining room table. The screen read "Mary." *Finally.*

"Hello, sweetheart."

"No, I'm afraid not," a man's deep voice replied. "Nick, it's Kent Huffman."

"Oh . . . Kent. I was expecting Mary."

"That's what I'm calling about," Kent said.

"Why are you calling from her phone? Has something happened to her?"

"Mary will be fine. Do you have time to talk?"

"She'll *be* fine? What's *that* mean?"

"I'll get straight to the point. Can Mary count on you?" Kent asked.

"Absolutely, anything. Where is she?"

"If you meet me at nine tonight, I can explain everything. You got a pen? Please write down this address. It should take you about twenty minutes to get there."

Nick wrote down the address. Being without Mary, even for this short time, made the world less to live in.

THREE MINUTES BEFORE nine o'clock Nick pulled over to view the address on a well-lit sign. In big black lettering the sign read:

Orange County Behavioral Institute
For a Better Living

This has to be a joke, he thought. *I've driven down this street a thousand times and never noticed this place. Nice frickin' observation, Detective.*

An eight-foot-high white stucco wall hid the property from view. Farther down the block, he found the main entrance. He drove up to a guardhouse.

"Excuse me," Nick said, "I think I have the wrong address. Is this—"

"Mr. Pajak, we are expecting you. Please pull your car forward; the gates will automatically open, and then follow the road to the parking area."

The black iron gate rolled open.

"All right. Can you tell—"

"Sorry, sir. Please pull forward," the guard directed.

Nick parked next to a silver Bentley, one of only two cars in the visitors' lot. He sat in his car, leaning forward to look up at the massive building. It was an early 1950s three-story structure of stone and red brick. The front of the building was brightly lit with each window containing its own wire mesh covering. The facility reeked of old money.

He saw a lone man standing outside the building's main entrance. The man wore a dark fedora and a lighter-colored overcoat. The floodlights over the doorway cast multiple eerie shadows, concealing the man's features.

As he got out of the car, Nick's imagination raced.

What the hell is going on? Is this some kind of intervention? He thought of Mary and cringed, knowing what type of place this was.

When do you really know someone?

Thirty=eight

"Kent!" Nick yelled out.

There was no reaction from the man in the entryway.

Nick stepped up his pace and, once close enough, he saw that it was indeed Kent. He breathlessly extended his hand. Kent shook it. He looked uneasy, his lips narrowed, worry evident on his brow.

"I wasn't sure if you were going to make it," Kent said, releasing his hand. He immediately turned and started leading Nick inside.

"Sorry about that," said Nick, breathing harder than expected. "Lots of security around here." Nick had already connected the dots but couldn't bring himself to say it out loud. A set of glass doors slid open.

Kent didn't reply, glancing up at a camera above.

The calm that reigned outside disappeared once they were inside the doors. They walked down the lengthy hallway accompanied by the faint cries and shallow yelps of patients. Nick felt a sudden chill; the hair on the back of his neck stood up.

Surveillance cameras mounted at both ends of the hallway watched them as they approached the last door. A buzzer sounded, the door unlocked, and Kent, who seemed to know the routine, pulled the door open. On the other side was an oversized waiting room. The walls were painted a sterile high-gloss white, bare of artwork or paintings. The floors were luminous white vinyl, with gray and black speckles. There was an overpowering stench of bleach that caused Nick's eyes to water. It made him think of the untold suffering that violence can cause—the reason he detested the smell of all hospitals. He repressed the urge to throw up.

Against three of the walls were chrome-framed chairs upholstered in waves of orange and yellow fabric that looked as if it dated from the '70s. Interspersed among the chairs were small glass tables with shiny chrome legs. The layout had an oversanitized feel.

The receptionist was at the far end of the room, behind a large pane of glass. To the left of the glass was a solid metal door with a single peephole, no handle or hinges. Painted on the door were words that gave a clear indication of its purpose: NO ENTRY WITHOUT PROPER AUTHORIZATION.

"Here's as good a place as any," said Kent, placing his hat on the table next to him. "Have a seat. I'll let them know when we're ready."

"Ready?" Nick felt his heart pound.

Apart from the woman behind the glass, they were the only two in the room. Kent's chair squeaked as he adjusted his position.

"I don't know what Mary has told you about her condition—"

"Condition?" Nick repeated. He was full of questions and seemed to be only coming up with single words.

"Yeah, her condition. She *has* discussed it with you?"

Nick's lips tightened, and he ran his hands over his face and hair, exhaling loudly.

"Well, of course not," Kent paused. "Okay, now this is making more sense."

"What is this place?" Nick's voice rose, denying his knowing.

The receptionist looked up.

Kent interlaced his fingers and frowned.

"Mary's being held here for observation. She's been diagnosed with a bipolar disorder."

"Mary? Really? *My* Mary?"

"Yeah, *your* Mary," Kent said sarcastically. "Okay, I have to explain this thing right," he said to himself.

"Mary's been taking a mix of medications for some time . . . to keep herself, well . . . balanced. And for whatever reason, she stopped taking them. And when that happens, she can go a little sideways."

Nick rubbed his eyes.

"Her reasoning skills diminish, she's easily angered, paranoia can set in, and sometimes she hallucinates. Have you noticed a recent change in her behavior? Any emotional outbursts? Perhaps one minute she's sweet as pie, and then the next, she'll verbally attack you out of nowhere, as if she is running on pure emotion?"

"Hmm." Nick nodded once—more to acknowledge Kent than out of understanding what was being said. He was hung up on the phrases "mix of medications" and "keep herself balanced."

"And then there's her sense of reality," Kent continued, "or lack of it. She's always tweaked the truth a bit. But when off her meds, she makes up shit—and I mean *loads* of it. To tell you the truth, at one point I doubted you even existed. Angie always believed otherwise. Then, of course, you showed up on our doorstep yesterday, proving her right.

"You have to understand, when it came to Mary's unorthodox behavior, we've given her a pretty wide latitude. I'm not trying to justify myself, but she hasn't exactly been around lately. You know the old saying 'out of sight, out of mind.' Her absence gave Angie and me a break. Anyway, she has talked about you, lunch dates—that sort of thing."

Nick stared into the air, listening.

"The doctors think she's been off her meds for quite a while—months, maybe longer. Then, this morning, I found out she stopped seeing her psychiatrist some time last summer. I take the blame on that one, since I pay for it."

Kent leaned forward, head bowed. "Yeah, there were some obvious telltale signs." He looked up, "But it's been years since her last bout. So, I thought . . . maybe, she's fine."

Nick remained silent, running his hands through his hair again.

"I admitted her last night," Kent said, "or was it early this morning?" He sounded tired.

"But it was Angie who took the brunt of it. Tough night for her. First, finding out that she's a stepmom, and then Mary came around banging on our front door, waking her up out of a sound sleep while I was out with Monika. Mary proceeded to yell and scream for me, scaring Angie half to death. Angie, who witnessed Mary's last meltdown firsthand, didn't open the door. She told Mary through the door to go home and I'd call her tomorrow. Thinking Mary had left, she went back to bed, but still frightened.

"A few minutes later, she heard glass shattering downstairs. She grabbed our gun and cautiously rushed down the steps. After turning on the foyer lights, she shouted out that she was armed. Hearing a squeaking sound coming from my office, Angie poked her head in. There Mary was, sitting in my chair, rocking back and forth, hands and arms bleeding, mumbling to herself. Angie ran back upstairs, grabbed our daughter from her room, and locked themselves in our bedroom. Then she called me, terrified. It was all I could do to talk her out of calling the police. Luckily, I had just dropped Monika off. I got home as fast as I could and . . . well, here we are."

Nick looked up, eyes vacant. He wasn't sure what to believe.

"Mary kept carrying on, demanding to know what you and I talked about," Kent said, pointing at Nick and back to himself.

Nick scowled. "Hmm . . . wow."

"Can you think of anything that might have set her off? I'm not blaming you. I'm only trying to figure out what happened. . . . What did you two fight about?"

"Nothing really. Though she did seem unusually quiet right after we left your house." Nick tilted his head in Kent's direction. Things started to click as he thought of some of her previous eccentric behavior.

"Then when we were at Cooks Corner she hurled a few accusations my way. I told her that she needed to calm down."

"Huh. Telling Mary what to do," Kent said grimly. "How'd *that* work out for you?"

"Yeah," Nick said bitterly.

"Are you two really engaged?"

"Sure, or at least up until today."

Kent blinked and exhaled hard.

"A while back, I asked her about the diamond ring she was wearing. She told me to keep the hell out of her business. That she could live her life the way she wanted and with whoever she wanted. I should've known something was wrong right then." Kent looked lost in regret.

"Did she ever say anything about our mother?"

"Not much," Nick said. "A little family history here and there, and she did show me *the book*."

"What book?"

"The big brown leather one. I believe she called it the *Legacy* book."

"Are you serious?"

"Yeah. I've got it at home right now."

Kent rubbed his eyes. "I don't believe this. That book was the cause of her last stay here. And I got rid of that thing years ago." This time, Kent moved his hands through his thinning hairline. "'Black dreams . . . sound familiar?"

"Yeah, and the strangest thing—"

"Amazing. I can't believe it's happening again."

"Again? What, how many times has she been here?"

Kent appeared transfixed, as if hit by a bolt of lightning. Sadness filled his eyes.

"Well?" asked Nick.

"Damn it." Kent stood up and turned away from Nick, linking his fingers behind his head. "*The book*, the black dreams, they're all lies. Just made-up shit."

He turned to face Nick. "Look, she's sick . . . and one of her major symptoms is having these pathological delusions. Meaning, she believes absolutely everything that comes out of her mouth as she says it. The hardest part is trying to extract the truths from her lies. Its mind-boggling how she's able to mix in concrete facts with what she thinks is real. She makes everything sound believable.

"I've helped her to live on her own, and up to this point, she's been pretty independent. Obviously, that's failed." Kent shoved his hands in his coat pockets.

Nick looked over at Kent. "What happened to her?"

"The best I can surmise comes from our mother—and there's plenty of skeletons in her closet too. The nightmares, black dreams, hallucinations, the lying, were all triggered when Mary saw some woman die. She was maybe six or seven at the time. She was with *her* father stuck in freeway traffic."

"Did you say her father?"

"Yes, her father and . . ." Kent stopped.

Nick blinked.

"Oh, you didn't know that either. . . . Mary's my half-sister, same mom, different fathers. Well, that's another story for a different time."

Nick looked disorientated.

"According to Mom, Mary and her father were stopped going south on the Five. And then from the opposite side of the freeway, a yellow VW bug jumped the median and crashed head-on into the car in front of them. The woman driver was thrown from the VW and smashed through their windshield, right in front of Mary. Obviously, the woman died on impact. From what was told to me, brain fragments had to be washed out of Mary's hair."

"Whoa . . . That's pretty traumatic for a little girl."

"For anyone. I'm pretty sure that's why she's hates yellow."

Nick connected the dots.

Both seemed to pause.

"Now that you know what you're getting into, here's the real question." Kent looked at Nick. "Do you *want* to see her? Can she count on you? I would completely understand if you didn't."

You can't be more full than filled.

Thirty-nine

The room was small: one window overlooked an interior courtyard; the walls were painted an olive green. Referred to as the "Avocado Room," it was only reserved for celebrities, prominent politicians, and other VIPs. Considered the *safe* room, there were no two-way mirrors or cameras. Privacy was its foremost feature.

In the center of the room was a square maple-wood table with four chairs. The overhead fluorescent lights were turned off in favor of a floor lamp in the corner that shed a forgiving indirect light. Ivory-colored curtains framed the heavily tinted window.

The director of the facility was an old fraternity brother of Kent's, who allowed him to reserve the room any time he needed, although the favors did not extend to a break on the astronomical cost of a stay.

NICK ENTERED THE room. The air was oppressively thick, which seemed to close over him like being caught in a wave's underlying pull.

Nick rubbed his nose. *I hate the smell of these places.* "Nice color," he said sarcastically, as part of his defense mechanism.

"You'll get used to it," said Kent, closing the door behind them. "Actually, it's kinda soothing."

They sat down at the table. Nick nervously tapped his finger and breathed through his mouth.

"Before she comes in, let's go over a few ground rules."

Nick leaned forward, feeling edgy.

"Number one, you need to relax." Kent paused. "You love her, right?"

"Yeah. But now—"

"No, none of this 'but now' nonsense. I thought this was settled. I can understand this is hitting you like a ton of bricks, but I don't have the time for you vacillating back and forth. You either love her, or you don't. So which is it?"

"I'm still here, aren't I?" Nick nodded. "Go on." He had never been wishy-washy when it came to making decisions. He blinked repeatedly.

"Good. Second, she's been pretty heavily sedated today, so she might not be all there. Try not to say anything that might upset her."

Upset her? Hell, I'm not sure if I even know who she is.

Nick leaned back, hands wet.

"Kent, you talked of my love for her. But what about her love for me? Is that real, or some fantasy world she's been living in?"

"That's the reason I called you. She does love you. And more important, she needs you right now, not tomorrow, after you've given it some thought. Not next month because all of a sudden, you feel guilty for whatever justifying reason you want to give yourself. But right now. That includes your full understanding and support. Eventually, everything will sort itself out. Just have some patience with her. That's all I'm asking. Now, take a minute and exhale."

Nick tried to compose himself. There were two quick raps on the door, and then it swung open. A male attendant positioned himself in the doorway—an intimidating, crew-cut, six-foot-six beast of a man. Mary stood outside in the corridor, her hair neatly combed and dressed in a blue hospital gown.

Mary stepped into the room.

"We'll be fine," Kent said to the attendant.

The attendant acknowledged Kent and shut the door, leaving the three of them alone. Mary took a seat at the opposite end of the table from Nick, as far away from him as possible, and then stared down into her lap. Kent sat between them.

"Mary, look at me," Kent said. "I brought Nick to see you."

Mary raised her eyes, focusing first on her brother, and then on Nick. A wisp of a smile crossed her lips, and then quickly vanished.

"Hey there, sweetie." Nick forced a smile.

Mary's eyes narrowed. "Why are you looking at me? What? I must look like a mess. Don't."

Nick gazed into her eyes, trying to find her.

"You never did say too much. And the things you did are running through my head like ripples from a stone thrown into lake. Always, endless. . . . Can you stay awhile? You've come for me? How lovely." She smiled.

Nick glanced at Kent and whispered, "The medication?"

"There aren't any secrets in this room," Kent snapped. "Mary, Nick needs to know if you're feeling better because of the medication."

Mary's focus remained on Nick.

"I want to go home, Nicky. Please, Nicky, take me home now. I'm scared and want to be with you."

"Now, Mary, you know better," said Kent. "We can't do that tonight. Maybe tomorrow. We'll see then."

"Nicky?" Mary's focus remained on Nick, seeking a different answer. Nick said nothing and gave Kent another quick glance.

"I'm sorry to put you through this," Mary said. "All right, yes, I didn't tell you . . ." she frowned with tightened lips, "everything . . . I wanted to. But I was afraid, terribly afraid you wouldn't love me anymore. Please, still love me."

Mary scooted her chair forward and wiped away an encroaching tear which was quickly replaced by another. Kent stood up and pushed in his chair.

"You two need to talk. I'll be outside," Kent said. "And, Mary, only the truth now; he needs to know. And no more talk about going home tonight. You got it?"

"Uh-huh," Mary looked away, and then down into her lap again.

"Nick, just knock when you're done," Kent said, as he gave the door two swift raps. It immediately opened, and Kent left without looking back.

Nick immediately got up and took the seat next to Mary. He leaned forward, resting his elbows on the table. He ran his hands through his hair, and then rested them on the table. Mary sat up straight, hands clasped together in her lap, like she was in church.

"I'm not sure what to say," Nick said.

"I messed it up pretty good, didn't I? How could you possibly ever love someone like me? What a horrible person I am."

"Mary, don't talk like that. How about we start by working on getting you well, okay?"

Mary bent forward, reaching for Nick's hands, palms up. He hesitated, then placed his hands in hers.

"Sweetie, all I ever wanted was honesty between us," Nick said.

Mary let go of his hands.

"You're using this as an excuse not to love me anymore, aren't you? You're giving up on me. Fine, here's your out. You can quit pretending you care and give me the truth." Mary began to cry silently, retreating to her stiff, upright position.

"Truth? Really, Mary?" Nick's voice rose. "You're asking *me* about truth? Try looking in the mir—"

Nick abruptly stopped remembering what Kent had asked of him. He leaned back in his chair, unsure.

"You didn't answer me," she said, voice quivering.

Nick said nothing.

"Oh, please, Nicky, you can't be that man with a hidden heart anymore. I hoped I had enough love for both of us. I was wrong." Her expression shifted abruptly to anger. "You should go. I don't want you anymore either."

Expressionless, Nick got up and went to the door. He knocked twice, and it quickly swung open. He turned back to Mary.

"Look, I fell in love with you. No pretenses, no lies. It was only me. I'm not sure who you are."

Mary sat silent.

The door closed, leaving her alone.

Once outside, Nick leaned back against the door. His mind was in a civil war against his heart. There was a thump sound and Nick felt the door vibrate against his body. A few seconds passed, then he heard a cry from Mary from the other side of the door.

"No no no. I'm sorry, please don't go. I didn't mean that," she whimpered. Then louder, "Oh, Nicky, come back; take me with you. I'll be good. I really will. Please, Nicky."

Too late. He had heard, but still he walked away.

I'm just a man—not a hero.

Forty

Nick woke up late the next morning, hurting all over. His back ached from sleeping in a contorted position on the couch, his head was pounding—actually, it was more of a continuous throb that worsened with every heartbeat. The effort of getting off the couch and making his way to the kitchen triggered reverberating pain that bounced inside his skull like a game of ping-pong.

He sat down, propped his elbows on the kitchen table, and rubbed his temples.

"What in God's name was I thinking?" he said out loud.

He remembered.

Nick bowed his head in remorse. He knew drinking wasn't the answer, but it seemed like such a good idea at the time— like every time. And it did dull the sting of her lies and of coming to grips with her mental illness. The hangover was a reminder of what he was trying to forget.

He raised his bloodshot eyes and stared at the kitchen sink. The slow, constant drip of the faucet was torture. A lone, empty Crown Royal whiskey bottle lay on its side on the table, a quarter-sized pool of whiskey below its mouth. He had no memory of opening it.

He noticed several crumpled pieces of paper scattered about on the floor.

I hate this! he thought.

He walked, a little wobbly, and retrieved only three of the balled-up scraps. He settled himself in the next room, in his leather chair, and uncrumpled the sheets of paper. One by one, he flattened one on top of the other. Placing them on his right thigh, he read the first:

Dear Mary,

Or maybe I should address this "To whom it may concern," because I feel like I don't even know you. Was it you who whispered I love you to me while we made love, or someone else? Are you even sure you know what love is? I believe all relationships should start with honesty. It did on my part.

Yet, I sit here alone, still wanting you.

Nick stopped reading and recrushed the paper, tossing it back on the floor. He picked up the next one.

Tonight, I didn't recognize you. Was that who you are?
Your brother told me things, things that not only shocked me—

Nick didn't finish reading it. That one ended up back on the floor as well.

He read the third sheet—it had one sentence—four words. He read it a second time and looked up, tears forming in the corners of his eyes. Nick pressed the sheet of paper to his chest as if it were Mary herself.

IT TOOK HIM minutes to get ready. He got out his best suit and the Vitaliano Pancaldi tie he had bought for their first date. Before leaving, he stuck the note on the refrigerator door with the "I heart San Francisco" magnet from his sister Pam.

The note read:

What would love do?

A sacrifice is only a sacrifice if it hurts.

Epilogue

Hearts, rings and time . . .

PULLING THE SHEET off him, Mary rolls over. Feeling the morning chill on his now bare chest, Nick opens his eyes. The sun shines through the gaps in the drapes, throwing stripes against the far wall. Turning toward her, he gently places his hand on her hip.

"Hey, sweetie, need a little warmth over here."

She releases the sheet and inches her bare back against his body. Not exactly what he meant, but vastly better.

"Morning, handsome." Mary snuggles closer. "I love you."

"Love you too." Nick chuckles to himself. "You ready for some coffee?"

"Nope. I'm happy right where I am."

This is their new morning ritual.

A LOT HAD changed over the past eighteen months. It started the day Nick plucked her out from the obscurity of the hospital and brought her home. His once-unused guest room became hers, though not for long. His bedroom was much more comfortable for her. In spite of what he had come to know and continued to learn of Mary's exploits: the delusions, her book of a family's phantom legacy, and even her intentional deceptions, he wanted her.

In the first few weeks, he worked with Kent and the doctors to establish a sense of normalcy. Every morning, at breakfast, while pretending not to watch, Nick made sure Mary took her medications. Twice a week, he drove her to the psychiatrist and waited patiently for the end of the session, sipping a cup of Starbucks coffee and reading the newspaper. Sunday mornings were church services, and later, dinner with Kent and Angie. Routine, routine, routine.

Mary came back to him one day at a time. Initially, she exhibited paranoia, crying out endlessly that Nick would someday leave her, like all men in her past. He steadfastly replied, "Oh, my sweet Mary. What would love do? That's right. Stay . . . always." His words were greater than himself.

There were days Nick struggled. It was tough trying to convince her of his devotion, especially when he doubted it himself at times. Twice he questioned if he had made the right decision. Yet, on both occasions, he found himself sitting at the kitchen table, staring at the note still posted on the fridge. It called for his measure as a man.

He reminded himself, *When you're at ground zero, a step in any direction is a step forward.*

Eventually, Mary's horror of abandonment subsided, only manifesting as infrequent outbursts of insecurity. Nick remained as a steady, guiding force, and hated it when Mary would say that she was worthless without him. Over time, Mary's confidence returned, revealing her true nature, without fear, with total clarity. Nick fell in love all over again.

When Nick testified at Stephanie's murder trial, Mary chose to stay home. She told Nick he needed to resolve his own guilt issues about Stephanie's death. And her being there wouldn't help. Mary was right.

He spent five days at the trial, finding out more about the killer than he wanted to. Russell Lynch, a victim of the system, was abused as a child, beaten, and surrendered up to social services at age twelve. By the time he became an adult, he had turned to crime and drugs. He perpetuated the stereotype of someone coming from a bad family and fulfilling a worse life. Lynch was convicted of voluntary manslaughter and sentenced to twenty years in prison. There, he would have plenty of time to work out his control obstacles.

Kent checked on Mary only once during Nick's absence. She seemed happy and stable.

After six months, Kent rented out Mary's old house. Kent had originally bought the place for her. Unfortunately, it had only enabled Mary to do nothing for years.

During her journey back, certain truths gradually came out. Mary didn't work for Kent. She never had. The night that Nick made his first call to Kent happened to be one of those rare times she actually checked on the kids for her brother. Mary explained that she wanted to sound important and never realized how that one little lie would roll downhill, picking up more lies, eventually becoming an avalanche enveloping her. Once she met Nick, she became addicted to him. That never changed.

Then there was the *Legacy* book—its mere existence haunts Kent. After Mary's last stay at the hospital, he personally tore out each page, tossing them one by one into the fireplace. He swore he watched them burn to ashes. Yet, a year later, the book reappeared again, this time on Nick's bookshelf. It was even bigger and more expansive than before. Mary, to this day, would not offer any explanation.

The contents of the book, in Nick's view, presented a greater mystery. Most of the entries were pure fabrication. The veracity of others is unclear, and still, some were reasonably plausible.

The chapter about the man who died in the hospital, the sheet covering his all-black face—not true. Mary did have an abortion at sixteen—the baby's gender, however, was never disclosed to her. Grandmama Matos did give Mary a copy of their family tree three days before her death. But it was only three notebook pages long, not an entire book, and there was no mention of any family curse. Mary's twisted logic and imaginative talents, intertwined with genuine facts, made the impossible sound possible.

The chapter regarding her Grandpa Heil's death was absolutely true. He died exactly as she had written, in a chair, before dinner, though the timing of her composition was suspect. Mary's version of the story shifted over the course of months, as she continued to improve.

Like Kent, Nick has his own paradox of the *Legacy* book to deal with. He remains deeply disturbed by the one black dream involving himself. That morning, Mary had called him hysterical, insisting darkness was coming his way, and hours later, he learned of Stephanie's murder. Things of that nature are not mere coincidences. And the simple explanation of Mary being off her meds didn't cut it for him. Nick had come to believe that she has a special connection to another plane, conceivably even the spiritual dimension. The *Legacy* book may be filled with mounds of manufactured falsehoods inspired by chemical imbalances, imagination, or gifts of prophecy, but whatever it is, when it came to dreams involving Nick, he wanted to hear about it.

They were married on a Wednesday morning at ten a.m.—not on Grandmama Matos's birthday. An odd choice, but that's Mary. She felt only their genuine friends and family would show up on a workday. Her thought was that people don't take time off work for just anybody. Nick was surprised when over a hundred guests RSVP'd.

Monika was Mary's maid of honor. Nick's sisters were the two bridesmaids. Monika and Mary originally got together at Nick's insistence. Without him, they were more likely to talk freely between themselves and resolve any lingering problems. Alone, they hit it off. Mary's jealousy never resurfaced. Monika calls Mary every time she comes into town.

As to the gold ring which started Nick's journey, it was given to Monika. No one understands how it miraculously appeared on Opal's grave marker years after Kent had left it there. Monika wears it daily as part of a necklace.

Nick smiles. "How about we have breakfast at the beach this morning?"

Mary rolls over to face him. "That sounds wonderful. But we have to find a new spot. You know they closed our favorite breakfast joint?"

"Yeah." Nick thinks for a moment. He brushes a few strands of hair from her eyes. "Then we'll just have to find another place. A better one."

"That's so you. Like with us, second time around and not afraid to try something new."

"Oh, Mary, I've never considered you second to anything. You're the thing I've been preparing for my whole life."

Mary's eyes sparkle, "Nicky, you do say the sweetest things. . . . I'm finally home. A real home—where I belong."

She was a star that didn't trust her own light . . . until now.